THE
BREAKTHROUGH

Center Point
Large Print

Also by Will Cook and available from
Center Point Large Print:

Bandit's Trail

**This Large Print Book carries the
Seal of Approval of N.A.V.H.**

THE
BREAKTHROUGH

WILL COOK

CENTER POINT LARGE PRINT
THORNDIKE, MAINE

This Center Point Large Print edition
is published in the year 2020 by arrangement with
Golden West Literary Agency.

Originally published in the US by
The Macmillan Company.

The text of this Large Print edition is unabridged.
In other aspects, this book may vary
from the original edition.
Printed in the United States of America
on permanent paper.
Set in 16-point Times New Roman type.

ISBN: 978-1-64358-579-6 (hardcover)
ISBN: 978-1-64358-583-3 (paperback)

The Library of Congress has cataloged this record under
Library of Congress Control Number: 2019957038

THE
BREAKTHROUGH

1

Charlie Two-Moon was born on the reservation and he grew up on the reservation and did not really know what the world was like until he joined the army and went to France to fight and bleed, and there he discovered a singular thing: that he was like all other men except that he had no luck at all.

He was twenty-three when he came back from France, one leg still in a cast, a bit of shrapnel still in his arm, but these things did not bother Charlie Two-Moon. He had been a brave man and although he did not mention this, the knowledge was there and he held himself straight because of it. Charlie Two-Moon was tall, a bit over six foot, and very slender. He had a thin, gaunt-cheeked face, deep brown eyes and Indian hair, black and straight.

The people in town held a dance for the boys who returned and Charlie Two-Moon attended this, although he spent all the time standing there, smiling woodenly, watching the others have a good time. They were all polite to him; men shook hands with him and told him they were glad he was home, but he knew what they meant, that his home was thirteen miles out on the old fort road.

His home was the reservation.

Before the dance ended, Dr. Oswald Carney drove him out there and for a while they rattled along in Carney's car without much talk and, because he was a white man, Carney couldn't stand this. He said, "How did you like the army, Charlie?"

"It was good," Charlie Two-Moon said. "The war was bad, but I liked the army."

Carney smiled and shook his head. "I was in the Spanish-American War. Never liked any of it." He looked at Charlie Two-Moon. "I suppose you'll marry and settle down now."

"There's no hurry," Charlie said. "I'd like to buy some land."

"Well, you've got ninety acres on the reservation."

"I meant land that wasn't reservation," Charlie said. He turned his head and looked at his friend. "You don't think I should?"

"Charlie, this is a free country, or so I keep reading in the papers," Carney said. "If you want a farm off the reservation, then buy it. Got any money?"

"I saved nearly all my pay," Charlie said. "Nearly three hundred dollars."

"That won't buy much of a farm," Carney said. "Take two thousand anyway."

8

"That's a lot of money," Charlie Two-Moon said and rode a way in deep thought. Then he reached down and pulled the emergency brake and the car stopped.

Carney said, "What the hell did you do that for?"

"Turn around. Take me back to town," Charlie said.

"Aw, come on, Charlie. All your relatives are waiting to see you. Hell, you'll miss the dancing and whoop-up."

"Take me back," Charlie Two-Moon said. He turned sideways in the seat. "Doctor, you're my friend. Without you I'd have finished four grades at the agency school and herded sheep the rest of my life. But you wanted me to come to town, to go to high school, and I did. Afterward there wasn't any place to go but back on the reservation and it was not easy, with my uncles and cousins constantly throwing it up to me how I had wasted myself." He shook his head sadly. "I suppose they wanted my sheep to get fatter, my grass to grow thicker because I'd graduated from high school. Doctor, when I went to the recruiting station to sign up, the sergeant expected me to make a mark. He didn't expect me to write. Then when I said I'd gone through high school, an officer came over and talked to me and I wasn't an Indian anymore. You know what I mean?"

"I do know, Charlie. I really do."

"That's why you've got to take me back to town, to the depot."

"What are you going to do, Charlie?"

"Go back in the army," Charlie Two-Moon said. "They pay every month. When I save enough money, I'll come back and buy my farm."

"Hell, I'll loan you the money," Carney said.

Charlie Two-Moon shook his head. "I'll earn it myself." Then he smiled. "You know, in my company there were only eight guys who'd finished high school?"

"I wish I had your guts," Carney said and turned the car around.

He caught the night train out, the westbound, and he knew where to go, and the army was happy to get him back because he'd been a good soldier. This time, because he was thinking of Dr. Oswald Carney, he signed up in the Medical Corps and was assigned to a hospital in the Canal Zone.

The army suited Charlie Two-Moon because it was a place where he could work and mind his own business and be rewarded for it, and he made corporal on the second year, and sergeant on the last year of his enlistment.

Once he came back on leave, stayed a few weeks, then went back to the army, signing over for another three years. He served it to the day, took his discharge, and came back to stay.

No one paid any attention to him when he got

off the train, older, heavier, more deliberate in his ways than he had ever been. The town had changed, grown, improved itself, yet he recognized it, did not feel out of place in it.

Dr. Carney still had his offices over the bank and he went up the stairs and the nurse had him wait; she thought he was a patient and treated him rather coolly and he knew what she was thinking; she was wondering why he didn't go to the reservation doctor.

Finally Carney came out and saw him sitting there, and he looked quickly at the nurse and said, "Ella, why the devil didn't you tell me—" Then he saw no point in going on with it and took Charlie Two-Moon by the arm. "For heaven's sake, come in, Charlie. My God, it's been a long time!" Just before he closed the door, he said, "No patients and no calls, Ella." Then he motioned Charlie Two-Moon into a chair. "You've put on a little weight, Charlie. Good solid weight. A little more serious around the eyes. Out for good?"

"For good," Charlie Two-Moon said. "I've come back to buy my place."

"Well, land's gone up in value. I don't think you could buy a decent piece for less than thirty-five hundred dollars," Carney said.

"I have a little over eight thousand dollars," Charlie said.

Carney whistled softly. "There must have been some good poker games coming your way."

"Gambling was too risky," Charlie Two-Moon said. "Soldiers are usually broke three days after payday, so I would loan them money. Not much, but five or ten dollars." He smiled. "In the army if you loan five, you get back six. Twelve for ten. It seems to be the rule. So I have over eight thousand." He took out a pack of cigarettes, offered one to the doctor, then gave him a light. "I learned a lot in the army, more than just how to make money. I've been studying. They have a lot of books."

"Like what?"

Charlie Two-Moon shrugged. "About farming and livestock and raising crops. I want to get me a place."

Carney looked at his watch. "It's close enough to noon. Suppose I go with you and we'll see Mortenson at the bank."

"I can do this alone if you're busy," Charlie said.

Doctor Carney laughed. "Hell, can't you let a man sneak out of his office once in a while?" He got up and opened the door and they stepped into the reception room. "I'm going to the bank," Carney said, and they went down the stairs together.

Charlie Two-Moon understood why Carney had come along; alone he would have been passed from one junior clerk to the other, but no one would do that to Carney, and when they were ushered into Mortenson's private office, he understood that it was Carney who was being invited and that he was along as a guest.

Mortenson was as Charlie remembered, only a little fatter. The banker shook hands with Carney and then looked at Charlie. "Two-Moon, isn't it?" He smiled at Carney. "Been losing many patients lately?"

"I'm down to about two a week," Carney said. "You get more skillful as you get older." He sat down and crossed his legs. "Charlie's come back from the army and would like to buy some property."

Mortenson nodded. "Don't you have some reservation land?"

"It's poor land."

"Well, it was free," Mortenson said.

"Nothing is free," Charlie Two-Moon said. "I want to buy some property."

"I see," Mortenson said. "Well, there are a few places for sale. Money's tight, you know. Times haven't been good. Have you been out to see your people yet?"

"No," Charlie said. "I haven't seen them for three years. A few days more won't matter."

"I see," Mortenson said again. "Well, I have forty acres near the old—"

"That's not large enough," Charlie said.

Mortenson had been interrupted and he didn't like it, not even when his peers did it, and he

13

considered himself as having very few of those. "I have an eighty-acre piece west of town. The house is in pretty bad shape and the barn—"

"I remember that place," Charlie said. "Ten acres is rock."

"You never seem to let me finish," Mortenson said mildly.

"There was no need to," Charlie said. "The last time I was here I noticed the old Robins place by the river. Tenants were farming it when I went out there. It looked like they were barely making the taxes. Then coming in on the train, I saw it from the coach window. It looked deserted."

Carney smiled. "Well, Milo, you can't say that he's blind."

Mortenson didn't appreciate the joke. He said, "That's a hundred and thirty-five acres of fine bottom land. No, I couldn't put a loan on that. There's forty-three hundred dollars on it now. With back taxes that I've advanced, I'd have to get five thousand." He shook his head. "As I said, Two-Moon, money is tight. Now about the forty acres near the old—"

"I'll pay cash," Charlie Two-Moon said quietly.

Carney folded his hands and waited and Mortenson sat there looking at Charlie Two-Moon, then color came into his fat cheeks and he said, "Where in hell did you get that kind of money? I never knew an Indian yet who had a pot to—" He clamped his jaws shut.

14

"Cash," Charlie Two-Moon said and reached under his shirt for his money belt. He counted out the five thousand in neat piles and let them lay on Mortenson's desk.

The banker said, "It's near noon. Suppose I draw up the papers around one-thirty?"

"That's fine," Charlie said mildly. "Could I have a receipt? As you say, money is tight and if anything happened to that, I don't quite have another five thousand to cover it."

Almost angrily, Milo Mortenson wrote out the receipt, and Charlie Two-Moon put it in his pocket, nodded his thanks, and left the office. After the door closed, Mortenson said, "The brassy sonofabitch. I never knew it to fail. Give an Indian a dollar and he wants to rub your face in the dirt." He glared at Oswald Carney. "What the hell do you see in him anyway? You've always taken his side."

"I see a man," Carney said. He got up and put on his hat. "The man I see is quite possibly the man I've never been and never will be. He walks tall, Charlie does. You ought to try it some time, Milo."

"Don't bandy words with me," Mortenson snapped. "By golly, the sheriff ought to look into this. He didn't get that money honestly."

"Don't be a fool," Carney said. "He got that money more honestly than you ever got yours, or I ever got mine. The night he came back from

15

the war I drove him out to the reservation and we got to talking. He wanted to buy a place then, had saved his money for it, but he didn't have enough. So he had me turn around and take him to the depot and he put in six years in the army to get the money. You know why, Milo? Because the army didn't care whether he was an Indian or not."

"All right, all right," Mortenson said, waving his hands. "So I let my prejudice show. But how's this going to look? Robins couldn't make a go of the place; it was just too much for him, and now an Indian comes along with cash and buys it. You know, there are others around here looking at that place."

"Why don't you sell it to them?" Carney said. "Let me tell you, Milo. Because they don't have the old bucks in the hand, that's why." He wiggled his finger under Mortenson's nose. "And while we're on the subject of Robins, let me point out that the place wasn't too much for him. Robins lost it because he's a lazy old duffer who thought he could throw seed on the ground and sit on his porch and watch it sprout."

Mortenson leaned back in his huge chair. "You've always been on the side of that Indian, Oswald, and I've always wondered why. You brought him into town, let him stay at your place while he went to high school. A lot of people have been curious about that. You want to know some of the rumors I've heard? Some say that he was fixing you up with a squaw out on the reservation." He looked at Carney. "Doesn't that make you mad?"

"No," Carney said.

"Well, aren't you going to deny it?"

"It wouldn't do any good if I did," Carney said. "Milo, you and a lot of people resented it when Charlie Two-Moon came to town to get an education. If he'd been black, it wouldn't have been any worse. Well, he took the worst your damned kids could hand out. He went through four years as alone as a man can be, and he asked for no favors and damned sure never got any. This isn't my country, Milo. I didn't come here like your father did, a sooner, and run all the Indians out. Unlike you, I don't live from day to day knowing they've got a reason to hate me."

"I don't give a damn what they hate," Mortenson said, blowing out a disgusted breath. "But you mark my words, Oswald, there'll be trouble over this. That Indian belongs on the reservation and the sooner he goes back there, the happier he'll be."

"No," Carney corrected. "You mean, the better off you'll be. You know, I offered to loan him money six years ago, but he wouldn't take it." He turned to the door and stood with his hand on the knob. "Better take care of that five thousand dollars, Milo. It isn't often you get cash these days."

17

"I can't understand why I don't hate you," Mortenson said.

Carney shrugged. "Well, we've known each other a long time, Milo, and I guess you know a lot of what I've said is true. The only difference between you and me is that you can't afford to always stand by the truth. Being a doctor, I have an advantage; they call me when they're sick whether they hate me or not."

"People respect and admire you," Mortenson said. "You ought to think of that, Oswald, before you take sides." He picked up the money and came around his desk. "Two-Moon belongs on the reservation. It's a fact and we can't do anything about it." Then he laughed. "Let's get some lunch."

"I was hoping you'd ask," Carney said, and they went out together. Mortenson stopped at the clerk's wicket, spoke to him, gave him the money to put away, and left instructions to have the deed ready by the time he got back. Then he went to the door where Carney waited, and they walked on down the street to the Hunter House.

All the influential men in town ate there.

2

Charlie Two-Moon walked the three miles from town and when he reached the gate leading to the barnyard and house, he stopped and looked at what he had bought. The house was not large, a frame, four-room place with a screened back porch and a stone path leading to the well twenty yards beyond. Trees shaded the house and there was a patch of green grass around the place, and where it ended the barnyard began. He had a good barn and a stout pigpen and a brooder house and a shed to keep farm implements out of the weather. His fields were gently rolling, well fenced, and a row of tall, dense trees marked the boundary of his place at the river.

But it was a good place, what he wanted, and he walked to the door, took the key out of his pocket, unlocked it and went inside. The house had a closed, musty smell and he opened several windows to air it out. Dust lay heavy on the furniture and the curtains were dingy; he'd have to clean everything, scrub it from top to bottom.

A truck he'd hired in town was going to bring his lockers from the depot, and the supplies he'd ordered at the store, and while he waited, he moved from room to room, taking a mental inventory. The Robinses had taken only their clothes when they left; dishes and some canned food and bars of half-used soap and their accumulated untidiness remained behind, and this irritated Charlie Two-Moon for he was used to living half-man, half-pig, and he had learned to hate it. That was the Indian way and he supposed that was why he wanted this farm, to work it well, to show people that he didn't have to live like that.

The delivery truck was late, but he expected that, and when it did arrive in late afternoon, Charlie Two-Moon had all the furniture moved into the yard, the rugs well beaten, and the kitchen scrubbed from top to bottom.

He helped the delivery boy unload, and the truck went back to town, and Charlie Two-Moon cleaned all the lamps, filled them with fresh kerosene and lit them, and went on working. He stored the food he had ordered, stacked the hand tools on the screen porch, put his trunks inside, and went on working.

He thought he'd like the southeast bedroom for himself and cleaned it thoroughly, made the bed and turned in for the night. Although he was tired, sleep did not come quickly and he lay there listening to the sounds, of a tree branch, wind-stirred, gently scraping against his roof, and the frogs along the river; these were all night sounds when a house was quiet, sounds a man was supposed to listen to because they came when he had time to listen.

The first blush of sun woke him and he got up and dressed and had his breakfast made and was eating it when a car came down the road and turned into his place. Charlie looked out the kitchen window, then got up and went out the back door as Doctor Carney stopped and got out; he came to the house, saying, "I had an early call over at the Peterson place. Thought I'd drop in for coffee."

"You're more than welcome," Charlie said, holding the door open for him. "Care for bacon and eggs?"

"You've sold me," Carney said and put his bag aside. He sniffed. "Soap. I can't recall the place ever smelling so good." He sat down at the table and watched Charlie Two-Moon fix the meal. "Pretty far along in the year to put in any kind of a crop, Charlie. Made any plans?"

"I read in the Chicago paper that lambs and poultry are down," he said. "I guess I could buy and hand feed this winter and come out all right." He splashed grease over the eggs. "How do you like 'em?"

"Turn them over," Carney said. "I can't stand snotty whites." He looked around the kitchen again. "Yes, sir, I've never seen the place so clean. The Robinses lived like Indians." After he said it, his eyes got round for he had surprised

21

himself, just letting it slip out that way. "Now why did I say a damned thing like that? Charlie, you know how I meant it."

"Indians are pigs; everybody knows that," Charlie said, bringing the plate to the table. He sat down across from Carney. "What's the talk in town?"

Carney shrugged and made a wry face. "Nothing much."

"I'd rather hear it from you," Charlie Two-Moon said.

"Why do you want to hear it at all?" Carney asked, half angry. "What does it matter what they think? They aren't half the man you are."

"It's always mattered," he said. "That's something I can't help. Doc, have you ever been to a whorehouse?"

Carney looked up quickly. "That's a hell of a thing to ask a man, Charlie."

"I asked because if you have, maybe you'll understand what I'm trying to say to you."

Smiling, Carney said, "Let's just say that I'm a man of the world. OK?"

"I wouldn't press an issue closer than that," Charlie Two-Moon said. Then his expression turned grave. "Sometimes I think it's funny, the notions white people have about Indians. I guess we're supposed to be able to stand in a cold rain and not feel it. Maybe we're not supposed to feel anything. I'll be thirty this winter, Doc, and you know, I've never slept with a woman. A couple of times in Panama I thought of doing something about that, and once some friends of mine and I went into town and we got in line and everything was all right until I got inside and the girls looked at me and I looked at them and I could just see the wheels going around in their heads. They didn't know what I was except that I had black hair and was plenty dark and they just figured that one of them was going to have a little bad luck that night. I turned around and walked out."

"You're a good man," Carney said simply.

This made Charlie Two-Moon angry and he stood up and waved his arms. "Good man, shit! I'm not a good man. Not a bad one either." He clapped both hands against his chest. "I just feel all locked up inside. Everything is wrong, every-thing I do. If I go back to the reservation, it's where I belong people will say, but they won't be glad I went. They'll say I'm just another lazy Indian living off their tax money. If I stay here they'll say I don't belong either. What am I going to do for a wife, Doc? Don't you think I want one?" He waved his arm in the direction of the reservation. "Am I going out there and buy one from her father and bring her here and have her cook out of one pot and pee in the corner because she can't understand what the backhouse is for?" He blew out a long breath. "I suppose folks think that because I went to school I've got big ideas about myself. Hell, it's not that, Doc. But I found out when I was a kid that there was more to the world than the medicine man said. There had to be ways of doing things other than what my father and his father had done."

He sat down and Carney finished his breakfast. "Charlie, you do what you think is right. That's all any man can do." He poured cream in his coffee and stirred it. "I always said that if a man could break away from his superstitious background, he could make out anyplace."

"What am I, an experiment to you?"

"No, no," Carney said. "It was just an observation. I don't give a damn how hard the teachers on the reservation work, the kids still go home and listen to their parents and the medicine man, and when the chips are down, they'll stake their faith on an idiotic omen instead of knowledge." He got up and took his plate to the sink. "Thanks for the breakfast. Anything I can send you from town?"

"I'd like to make up a list, if you could wait another ten minutes," Charlie said and tore off part of a sack. He wrote down his list, folded it, and handed it to Doctor Carney, then he walked out to the car with him.

After Carney drove away, Charlie Two-Moon began his day's work, cleaning the rest of the house and doing a large wash on the back porch. He washed the curtains and the small rugs, stopped briefly at noon for something to eat and worked on until dark.

He had said a lot more to Carney than he had meant to, but now that it had been said, he wasn't sorry for it. But if he had it to do over, he would have kept it all to himself. Somehow it embarrassed another man to hear those kinds of things; it was like crying without tears, and tears a man could forget but this would stick in the mind.

He felt an obligation, and a near sense of guilt because he had not gone to the reservation to visit his relatives, yet he told himself that he would once he got a little more settled. Only he knew this was not the truth. He wanted to put them all behind him, forget them, but he couldn't do that.

They came to see him, his uncle, Ed Lame Bear, with his family and their families, with their horses and tents and children and barking dogs and they camped in his yard, and that same day, his cousin, Tom Walks Far, showed up and he had fifteen people with him, and they built a fire in his barnyard and took all his smoked meat and had a feast and afterward there was dancing and all Charlie Two-Moon could do was to sit on his porch and hate them all.

Ed Lame Bear was an older man and he wore jeans and a bright shirt and a peaked hat with a blue feather in it and he was the leader and sat on the porch with Charlie Two-Moon.

"Why are you not dancing?" Ed Lame Bear asked. "Charlie Two-Moon is the best dancer on the reservation." He reached over and poked him in the ribs with his finger. "There are some pretty girls asking where Charlie Two-Moon is tonight. Why do you sit here on the porch like an old man?"

"Get your people off my property," Charlie said quietly.

"This very morning I said, we must go—" He stopped talking. "What did you say?" He put a finger in his ear and juggled it around. "My old ears are not—"

"There's nothing wrong with your ears," Charlie said. "You can hear a cigar butt drop in sawdust from across the street. Now get your people out of here. You come on my place, make a pigpen of my lawn and—"

"It is only grass!" Ed Lame Bear exclaimed. "There is much grass on the prairie. Why do you make so much fuss over this?"

"—and you ate up nearly all the provisions I put up for the winter," Charlie went on.

"Food! Food is to eat! Do you want it to spoil? Is it not our way to share with each other?" He spread his hands in bewilderment. "What is this strange way, Charlie Two-Moon? Is not what I have yours for the asking?"

"Just what have you got anyway? A filthy shack and a dozen sheep." He got up. "Are you

26

going to get 'em out of here or will I have to?"

"You would offend your people over a little grass and food?"

"Damn it, it's more than the grass and food," Charlie snapped. "But I don't suppose you can see that."

Ed Lame Bear stood up slowly. "I see much, Charlie Two-Moon. I see that you have turned your back on us. You have taken strange ways that I do not like."

"That's enough," Charlie said and stepped off the porch. The singing and dancing raised dust in his barnyard and they had taken down a few of the pickets of the fence for fuel for the fire, and when he saw this thoughtlessness, a dark anger came to his mind.

He saw Tom Walks Far dancing with a young girl, and he reached out and fisted a handful of Tom's shirt, halting his wild thrashing about.

Tom Walks Far looked at him and said, "I am glad to see you come to dance, Charlie."

"Dance, hell!" Charlie said. "You're going to dance right off my place and stay off!"

The words, the tone shocked Tom Walks Far, and then he saw Ed Lame Bear come up. "What is this, Uncle? Has there been something to drink besides water?" He looked at Charlie Two-Moon. "You look at me strangely, Cousin. Your hand still holds my shirt. I do not like that, Charlie." He looked at Charlie with his round, dark eyes and his expression was beginning to change, to grow hard. "We came in peace, to share your good fortune, Charlie. It was not known to me that you have grown selfish."

"You come on my place, pitch a camp and eat like pigs and you want me to be happy about it." He jerked on Tom Walks Far's shirt and spun him away. "Get out of here and stay out of here."

Ed Lame Bear moved first. He reached inside his shirt and brought out some socks and a spoon and a few other things he had stolen from the house, and he dropped these on the ground by Charlie Two-Moon's feet. They all followed this pattern, and each had something to drop and by the time the last of them had passed in front of him, there was a large pile in the yard, most of his silverware, and his dishes, and useless things that they stole only to be stealing something.

They broke camp, loaded their wagons and got on their horses and began to leave, then Tom Walks Far came back; he rode a calico pony and he wheeled it dangerously close to Charlie Two-Moon, then he leaned over to spit.

This was his mistake, thinking that Charlie was an Indian who would endure the insult for the privilege of returning it. Charlie jerked him off the horse, threw him to the ground, then yanked him erect and slammed his fist into Tom Walks Far's nose.

28

Blood flew and Tom yelled in sudden pain, and Charlie said, "You damned filthy Indian," and hit him again; he would have knocked him down if he had not been holding him.

Ed Lame Bear came back. "Let him go, Charlie Two-Moon."

It was the voice of authority running back to childhood and although he hated himself for obeying, Charlie let Tom fall, then stepped back.

"You have done a bad thing," Ed Lame Bear said sternly. "It will be discussed and decided upon."

"Discuss it all you damned please," Charlie said. "Get off. Stay off. What your tribal council decides doesn't concern me."

He refused to help Tom Walks Far on his horse, and he stood there while they left his place and the anger stayed with him, anger at himself, anger at them.

They were his people, his family, and he had pushed them away because they were not what he wanted them to be, because he was ashamed of them, embarrassed because they did not pretend to be anything but what they were.

I am not an honest man, Charlie Two-Moon thought as he turned to the fire to pour water on it. It bothered him, not to be able to think of himself as an Indian without shame. There was no reason to feel this reaction, no reason unless he alone gave himself the reasons.

As he went to the house, he thought: it's good that I live alone. I must do a lot of thinking and must find many answers before I'm truly a man.

3

Fred Teeter always brought his wife and boys into town on Friday night to do the weekly shopping, and he spent his time in Mel Allen's pool hall bellied up to the poker table. The state was "dry," but Allen always managed to have some bootleg beer hidden in the back room, and Fred Teeter would drink and play until midnight, then take his family home.

The card game was an hour old and Teeter had already made two trips to the back room. He played a sour hand, rode out two raises, then chucked it and leaned back in his chair. He was thin, thirty, dry-humored. All these men seemed thin, and somehow it went with their life, went with the land on which they lived, for the prairie was a thin place, thin on water, thin on crops too sometimes when the grasshoppers came and stripped it all. Their houses seemed thin, made of thin boards, and thin dust blew now and then and went through the thin cracks that no carpenter seemed able to close up. And in the summer the sun was thin, a bright, pale yellow, washed out in color and the heat was thin and piercing, going right through a straw hat or the weave of a man's shirt.

"I knew the sonofabitch all through school," Fred Teeter said. His voice was rather high-pitched, a sharp, penetrating voice. Two men playing pool looked up then went on with their game. "Sat right behind him the last year, looking at that black, shiny hair." He took out a sack of tobacco and rolled a cigarette. "You were in the same class as me, Mel. You never liked him either."

"It wasn't that I disliked him," Allen said. "It's just that I didn't have anything to do with him. You know, I leave people alone. A man can't be in business and taking sides all the time. Charlie Two-Moon never comes in here. He leaves me alone and I leave him alone." He took off his derby and scratched his prematurely bald head. "I've got three tens. Anybody beat that?" Nobody could so he raked in the small pot and anted a nickel.

"The thing that gripes me," Teeter said, "is that a man works his butt off farming, trying to get ahead and put some by so he can expand, and then some damned honyock comes along and buys right out from under you."

One of the other men looked up from beneath the tipped brim of his hat. "I never knew you wanted to buy the Robins place, Fred."

"Well, sure I wanted it," Teeter said. "Hell, who wouldn't want it, good bottom land like that."

"Wantin' something ain't the same as bein'

32

ready to buy it," the man said. He threw in his cards. "I guess I'll walk around a spell."

"That leaves us short-handed in the game," Teeter said.

"So it does," the man said and walked out of Allen's place.

He walked up and down the street on both sides and looked in some of the stores. He saw Teeter's wife sitting on the front porch of the hotel, as she did every Friday night, waiting patiently for her husband's pleasures to end. He had seen her sitting there before and it had never bothered him, but now he stopped and watched her without seeming to watch her at all. Pretty soon Teeter would leave the pool hall, with Allen, or with someone else, and they'd go out the back door and get into a car brought around to the alley and go out to the reservation to see what kind of a woman they could find, and afterward they'd come back and bathe in the back of Winkler's barbershop and then Teeter would get his wife and drive home as though nothing had happened.

It seemed strange to him that he had never thought of this before, but he supposed that was because he'd been a part of it and saw it only from one angle. Now, leaning against the feed-store wall watching Alice Teeter, he was struck sharply by the injustice of it, the shame of it.

He was prompted to move, and he stepped on down the street, stopping by the porch. He took off his hat and said, "Evenin', Miz Teeter."

She looked at him, erasing the faraway expression in her eyes. "Why, Jim Holbrook, I didn't see you standin' there." She was in her late twenties, still pretty, he thought, in a thin, worn way. Her hair was dark and he suspected that there was a trace of Cherokee blood in her, probably on her grandmother's side. She had a thin, oval face, and when she smiled some of the hard work written there was erased. "It's a nice night, ain't it?"

"A bit chilly, but nice," Jim Holbrook said. "Mind if I sit a spell? If it don't seem improper."

"Why, you're Fred's friend, Jim. Come on the porch." He sat down and held his hat in his hands. Holbrook was sandy-haired and his eyebrows were blond and thin so that at first glance it seemed that he didn't have any at all. His complexion was always red, made so in the summer by the sun and in the winter by the cold; he was a man who could never tan, alternating always between freckles and peeling.

"Fred's playin' cards," he said matter-of-factly.

"I know. Don't you always play?"

"Didn't feel like it tonight," he said. "I don't like too much talk when I play and some of the fellas was pretty windy. You know how they get some time, wound up so's they can't stop."

"Fred ain't much for talk," Alice Teeter said. "Sometimes he goes for days without speakin'. It used to bother me, when we was first married,

34

but now I kind of welcome it." She looked at him. "How come you never took a wife, Jim? You're a right handsome man."

"Aw, I ain't," he said.

"You are. I always thought so," she said.

He moved his head from side to side and shuffled his feet. "I wish you wouldn't talk like that. It don't seem right."

"Well, I tell the truth," Alice Teeter said. "I don't say things I don't mean."

"A pity everyone ain't like that," Jim Holbrook said. "But we just go on through life lyin' all we think we can get away with and hopin' we don't get caught. I guess that's the way we measure success, doin' all you can and not gettin' caught." He looked at her and changed the subject. "I don't see your boys about."

"They're over to the school yard playin' on the swings and teeter-totter. It's somethin' they look forward to each week, kind of like Fred looks forward to his poker game."

"And what do you look forward to, Alice? Sittin' on the hotel porch, waiting?"

For a moment she sat there looking at the people walking up and down the street. Then she said, "I don't mind waitin', Jim. It's what a woman does best."

"If you was my woman you wouldn't have to do it," he said quickly. The talk was a little bold and he got up and put on his hat. "I've said too

35

much. 'Night, Miz Teeter." Then he left the porch and walked rapidly down the street.

As he passed the hardware store he saw Doctor Carney at the counter and he turned back and went inside. Carney had paint cans and brushes and other bits of hardware stacked on the counter.

Holbrook said, "Painting your office, Doc?"

"No," Carney said. "Charlie Two-Moon wanted me to get this order filled." He looked sharply at Holbrook, then checked his watch. "Poker game broke up already?"

"I kind of got tired of it tonight," Holbrook said. "Fred Teeter was spoutin' off again. Just talk, but that's all it ever is with Fred. You get kind of tired of it after while."

The clerk came back with the list; he had checked off all the items. "I guess Charlie wants this delivered. Be another dollar."

"He didn't say anything about coming in after it," Carney said, "so I guess you'd better take it out to him."

"This will have to be cash," the clerk said. "The boss wouldn't like it if I—"

"He'll pay for what he gets," Carney said. "He always does." He looked at his watch again. "I'll see you later, Jim."

He left the store and walked to the corner and crossed over to the bank building and went up the steps to his office. He unlocked the door and lit the lamps, then went into the back room and unlocked the back door. Then he stepped out onto a small porch and looked at the dark base of the stairs that opened into the alley.

Fred Teeter came up and stepped inside. "You're on time, Doc."

"I try to be," Carney said dryly, "but most of my patients use the front door." He closed the door and motioned for Teeter to sit down, but the man shook his head.

Carney shrugged and said, "Suit yourself. Fred, you've got gonorrhea. There's no mistake."

"I've got what?"

"You've got the clap," Carney said. "A good dose. Why didn't you come to me before?"

"I thought it was a strain or somethin'," Teeter said, then clenched his teeth. "Goddamned Indian slut anyway." He sat down in the chair Carney had offered. "What do I do, Doc?"

"You'll have to submit to treatment and none of it's going to be fun," Carney said. "We'll have to flush you out with silver nitrate and try to dry it up. But you've got some restrictions that will have to be cut out." He leaned against a cabinet of instruments and looked at Fred Teeter. "You've got yourself in a mess. Maybe you don't know it, but you've probably infected your wife. I want her to come in for an examination."

"My God, I can't do that!" Teeter said. "You mean, tell her?"

"I don't see how you can avoid it," Carney

said. "You'll be wearing your penis in a bag for a few months at least. How are you going to hide that from her?"

"Jesus," Teeter said and put his head in his hands. "I ought to kill that slut for this."

"That's right," Carney said. "It's her fault." He made a wry face and lit a cigar. "I want your boys to come in for an examination too. You can communicate this from an outhouse seat, you know. If they've got it, I want to check it before it goes too far." He looked at Fred Teeter and puffed on his cigar. "You've done a fool thing, Fred. A damned fool thing. Now you've got to pay for it. Trouble is, innocent people will have to pay too. When was the last time you had intercourse with your wife?"

"That's a hell of a thing to ask a man," Teeter said.

Carney displayed his anger. "You stupid, arrogant fool! I'm your doctor and I've had about enough of you! Now I asked you a question and I want an answer."

Teeter shrugged and moved his head and made a face. "Night before last."

"I want her in here in the morning," Carney said. "You understand that?"

"Yeah, yeah, I understand," Teeter said. "Don't make such a big thing of it."

"I want her to bring the boys too," Carney said. "After each urination, they're to wash their hands thoroughly. If they transfer this to their eyes it's apt to blind them."

This shocked Teeter and he said, "God, I didn't know that."

"There's so much you don't know," Carney said. "Now take down your pants."

"Is this going to hurt?" Teeter asked.

"Yes, I'm happy to say," Carney said. "Lay down on that table."

"Well you could give me something if it's going to hurt," Teeter said.

"I could," Carney said and prepared a long syringe nearly the size used to inoculate livestock and Teeter's eyes got round.

"My God," Teeter said. "You're not going to poke that thing up me, are you?"

"Halfway to the heart," Carney lied calmly.

He treated Fred Teeter, washed his hands carefully with strong soap, then put on his coat and left his office. Teeter lay on the table, an arm flung over his eyes and sweat was still a slickness on his face.

The dirty bastard, Carney thought, just before he closed the door. He walked down the street to the hotel and found Alice Teeter still sitting there. The two young boys were playing on the far porch rail, pretending they were on horses and chasing Indians.

"May I have a word with you, Mrs. Teeter?" Carney said.

"Of course, won't you sit down. I don't know where Fred is but—"

"This is rather a delicate matter," Carney said. "I've already spoken to Fred. Fact is, I'm speaking for him now." Her expression was curious and this made it all the more difficult for him. "Mrs. Teeter, I've asked Fred to bring you and the boys to my office in the morning. I really believe that you have a—well, a social disease." She continued to look at him, her expression unchanged, and he knew that she didn't understand him. Carney glanced around and found no one in earshot, so he put it straight out to her. "Fred has the clap. I'm sure he's given it to you and the boys. I want you to come in tomorrow morning without fail. If he won't bring you, I'll come out to the farm and get you. This is most serious."

He thought for a moment she was going to fall for she swayed in the chair, then she caught herself, brought herself under control. "How—how did he get this?"

"I have no way of knowing," Carney lied.

"You know," she said. "And I think I know. I hear talk that a lot of the reservation Indians have it. Has Fred been going out there?"

"I didn't ask him that," Carney said. "I'm interested in the disease and the cure, not the cause or the circumstances of contraction of it. Alice, you will see me tomorrow, won't you?"

She nodded. "I was going to come in anyway in a week or so. I've missed two periods and been having mornin' sickness."

Carney closed his eyes for a moment as though asking God why this had to happen. Then he got up and turned to go and he would have if she hadn't spoken. "You tell Fred I want to see him. Is he in your office?"

"Yes."

"You tell him I want him to come here to me and look at me and tell me to my face where I failed him."

"I'll do that," Carney promised. "Alice, this is something Fred and you can work out together. He's made a mistake, sure, but—"

He stopped talking when she shook her head. "That would be true if Fred would ever admit to making a mistake. But he won't. You know why he won't? Because he can't see himself at all. He looks in a mirror and it's a complete blank. No, Fred will never see where he's done wrong. It's someone else. It always is. You'll see."

"The man's got to face up to the truth," Carney said.

"He won't," Alice Teeter said. "He'll find someone to blame. You've got to understand Fred. When he steps in manure, it ain't because he wasn't watchin' where he put his feet, it's because some stupid cow made a mess where he was liable to walk. You tell Fred I want to see him."

"Yes," Carney said. Then he turned off the porch and walked slowly back to his office, trying to let his anger cool before he stepped inside and looked at Fred Teeter.

4

Charlie Two-Moon had a lot of work he wanted to get done before the winter set in; he painted the house on the outside, two coats, and the barn got a coat of red and the roof was fixed, and he gave the inside of the brooder house a coat of coal oil and linseed oil to kill the chicken lice. He replaced the pickets that had been torn from his fence, erased all sign, all damage caused by his relatives from the reservation.

He was three weeks on the place and already it took on a different complexion, a look of prosperity, although he knew this was only looks. He'd start stocking when the snow fell, coast through the winter, pouring a little money into feed and silage, then in the spring work it for a profit.

The farm kept him going from dawn to dark and he hadn't been to town since his return, and he felt no desire to go in; he had replenished his food supply by giving the hardware store delivery boy his order, and the work kept him satisfied.

Each morning was turning progressively chillier, and there was a small rime of ice forming on the watering trough, and late at night his windows would steam over, especially when he had the fire in the living-room stove going good. He kept watching the sky for the first hint of snow, but it held off, and he needed the time for he had some outside work he wanted to do.

From the reservation road, a buggy came toward his gate, and Charlie stood in his yard as Jules Kerrick drove his rig by the big sycamores and stopped. Charlie walked over as Kerrick got down, then helped his wife.

Kerrick was forty, a man of dry expression. He raised his right hand and said, "How," and Charlie did the same, then they both laughed and shook hands. Kerrick said, "You didn't come to the reservation to see me, Charlie. Have you got something against Indian agents?" Then he turned to the woman. "Edith, you remember Charlie Two-Moon, don't you?"

She didn't, Charlie was sure, because he had met her only once, six years before, right after Kerrick brought her to the reservation. But she lied nicely and said, "Of course; how are you, Charlie?"

"Getting cold standing out here," he said. "Let's go into the house." He led the way, opened the door for them and they stepped inside. There was a fire in the living room and they backed up to it and toasted.

Jules Kerrick looked around and nodded, then said, "It's a home, Charlie. Nice. What I expected."

44

Edith Kerrick was looking at everything through a woman's eyes, the kind that searched out every speck of dust, every below-the-surface untidiness, and Charlie watched her, positive that she would find nothing that displeased her. Then she glanced at him and caught his study, and blushed. "I suppose you know what I was doing?"

"Yes," he said.

"I'm sorry."

"Don't be," Charlie said.

Jules Kerrick frowned pleasantly. "What the devil's going on here anyway?"

"For a bachelor," Edith said, "Charlie knows a surprising amount about woman's nature." She had a pleasant, round face, not beautiful or even striking, just pleasant, the wholesome attractiveness that would hold a man's interest when she was fifty. Her figure was full, rounded, plump, but not fat. She took off her gloves and hat, and laughed. "Now that I've been found out, I feel more at ease."

"I still don't know what the devil she's talking about," Jules Kerrick said. He rubbed his hands together briskly and laughed. "I wish I could afford an automobile, but not on my salary."

"You ought to take graft," Charlie said. "People will say you're a damned fool if you don't."

"They already say that," Kerrick admitted. "Or else they say I'm taking graft and salting the

45

money. I could use some coffee if you have any."

"Jules!" Edith said, surprised. "My, that's awful forward."

Kerrick laughed and Charlie said, "We've cut our palms and put them together. We're blood brothers."

"Not really," Edith said. "All right, I'll make the coffee. It'll give me a chance to snoop in the kitchen." She went to the hall archway, then stopped and looked back at Charlie Two-Moon. "And I *did* remember you from six years ago."

He let the surprise on his face betray him and she smiled then went on to the kitchen. Kerrick said, "By God, I like that woman, even if she is my wife." He brought out two cigars and a light and they sat down. "Can I turn to you for help, Charlie?"

"If you need it, Jules."

"I've got Indian trouble," Kerrick said.

"What is it this time?"

"Doctor Carney came out to see me three days ago. It seems that one of our sterling citizens has contracted a venereal disease and Carney wants the agency doctor to examine all the Indians on the reservation."

"That'll be quite a job," Charlie Two-Moon said, "but it's not a bad idea. Of course, you'll have to stop some of the men from town from coming out to the reservation for their fun. And how are you going to educate the girls to keep

46

them from taking fifty cents or two bottles of beer?"

Jules Kerrick shook his head and wiped a hand across his face. "Charlie, the whole thing, the hopelessness of it, really gets me. And then this has all come at a very bad time."

"How's that?"

Kerrick hesitated. "I like to leave a man's business alone, but there's a lot of blue smoke on the reservation, you know, a lot of medicine being made. Whatever happened between you and Ed Lame Bear is really your business, as long as it doesn't interfere with mine. But it has, Charlie. They're taking sides, Ed Lame Bear and Tom Walks Far on one side, with all their relatives, and the rest of the reservation backed over in the other corner."

"How does that hurt you, Jules?"

"Because we're friends. You know how they are, against you, and against your friends. I'd like to see you patch this up, Charlie."

"Bring gifts?"

"Well, it's the Indian way," Kerrick said. He looked up as his wife came in with a tray. She put it on a small table, then said, "I can see that you had to get right down to business, Jules."

"No sense beating around the bush."

They took their coffee and Charlie sipped some of his, then said, "It's not the kind I make."

"Well, thank goodness," Edith said. "I was

beginning to feel pretty useless." She looked at her husband, then at Charlie Two-Moon. "Should I go back in the kitchen?"

They laughed and the silence eased. Charlie said, "Jules, suppose I come out to the reservation and spend a day or so. Suppose I bring gifts and make up between my uncle and myself. Do you know what I'm buying? An open invitation for them to return the visit. Jules, I don't want my place torn up or littered up. It's as simple as that. When they come here, they've got to live my way, and act my way."

"You're asking the impossible," Kerrick said, "and you know it." He put his coffee aside and leaned forward. "Charlie, I don't want more trouble from anyone in town. Lord knows who got caught—Carney wouldn't tell me and I knew better than to make an issue of it, but if this gets out, and it's bound to, every damned self-styled dignitary in town is going to howl his head off. All this country was stolen from the Indians in the first place and every time they think of the reservation they remember it. They just don't want the Indians around."

"What's the answer?" Charlie asked.

"You're the answer," Kerrick said simply. "Get off the reservation, and stay off it. In time, they may all do that."

"We'll never live to see it," Charlie said.

Kerrick shook his head in doubt. "I don't know.

I wouldn't want to say that because I'm no longer sure of it. Charlie, it isn't enough that you got off the reservation. You've got to reach back and help others."

He thought about this, then looked at Edith Kerrick. "You're not a talkative one, are you?"

"I didn't think I should say anything," she said.

"I'm inviting you," Charlie said.

"All right, Charlie. We all have to have a Dr. Carney in our lives. Could you have made it without Carney?"

"Guess not," he said. "Let me think about it, Jules."

"Don't take too long."

"Why, I never do," Charlie said and drank the rest of his coffee.

Kerrick wanted to go outside and look around the place and Edith wanted to stay inside by the fire, so Jules Kerrick left and Charlie Two-Moon refilled his coffee cup because he couldn't think of anything better to do.

Edith said, "A wife would be a help to you, Charlie."

"The thought has entered my mind," he admitted. "Any suggestions or anyone in mind?"

"My," she said, "it is a touchy subject."

"Sorry. I didn't mean to sound edgy, but there's not much I can say. If I said I was looking for a nice Indian girl, it would sound as though my own people aren't good enough. If I suggested marrying a white woman, you might think I was going out of my class." He picked up his cigar, punched the ash, and rekindled it. "White men marry Indian women, but it's never the other way around. And I don't care to start any trends."

"I can't say as I blame you," Edith Kerrick said. "But I do wish you'd come out to the reservation, Charlie."

"We'll see," he said, then turned his head as Jules Kerrick came into the house.

"It's a good farm," Kerrick said. "Ready to go, Edith?" He helped her into her coat, and Charlie Two-Moon went outside with them. The horse was restless and eager to go and Kerrick didn't waste any time. When they turned out, Charlie waved and went back into the house because he was in his shirt sleeves.

He took the coffee and cups into the kitchen and washed everything, then put on a clean shirt and his coat and decided to go to town. He had a walk ahead of him but he didn't mind it, keeping up a steady pace, and he reached the main street an hour later. Curly Moss ran a combination livery stable and garage, and Charlie Two-Moon went there, spent some time dickering, and bought a wagon and team for three hundred dollars. He put the bill of sale in his pocket, got in the rig and drove in back of the feed store, and parked there.

A card game was in progress around a board placed on the end of a barrel, and the men looked up when Charlie Two-Moon came in. He knew them: Fred Teeter and Mel Allen and Al Winkler, the barber. Jim Holbrook was there, but he was standing out of the game; Pete Scarbrough, who owned the store, made up the fourth man at play.

Scarbrough said, "I'll be with you in a bit, Charlie."

"No hurry," Charlie said easily and leaned against the counter.

Fred Teeter looked up and grinned. "Take your time, Pete. Charlie's in no hurry at all."

Jim Holbrook had been paring his nails and he stopped that and put his knife away. He glanced at Charlie Two-Moon without seeming to and went on waiting. The cards went down, were looked at, and money went to the center of the board. Mel Allen and Fred Teeter exchanged brief glances, then Teeter threw in his hand and said, "My luck's turned sour all of a sudden." He looked around as though to see who to blame for this, and his eyes settled on Charlie Two-Moon. "Somehow I just can't picture you without a blanket wrapped around you."

"Try," Charlie said softly.

Teeter smiled and put his hands on the edge of the board. "I never liked you, Charlie."

"That's news?"

"Don't get smart with me," Teeter said. "I don't take it off any man, and surely not an Indian." He reared up and Mel Allen did the same and they started around both sides of the barrel, and then Jim Holbrook stuck out his foot casually and sent Allen asprawl. The man hit hard, rolled, and sat up.

Allen said, "What the hell did you do that for?"

"Stay out of it," Holbrook said quietly. "I won't tell you again."

The hardness was there in his voice and in Holbrook's eyes, and Allen got up and stepped clear. He dusted off his pants and said, "Sure. Sure, Jim. Hell, I was only—" He let the rest trail off and stood there.

Fred Teeter remained rooted, and Charlie Two-Moon said, "Well, what are you going to do, build a nest?"

Teeter's anger was a growl in his chest and he jumped Charlie Two-Moon, closing the distance with one bound, his arms swinging, fists doubled. Charlie ducked, whirled, pushed and hit at the same time, his fist smacking into the flesh and bone just behind Teeter's ear. It sounded like a man slapping a horse on the rump with a leather strap and Al Winkler winced and closed his eyes.

Teeter sprawled across the counter, bounded off, hit the floor, and lay there, moving, trying to get up, but too stunned to make it instantly. Charlie Two-Moon stood there, watching him, waiting for him, and thinking of his seven and a half years in the army where he had enforced the authority of his sergeant's stripes with his fists, and he felt sorry for Teeter, who lacked this experience, and relied only on his hate to make his fight.

"Are you going to get up or lay there?" Charlie asked.

"I'll get up," Teeter said raggedly, and did, and he came in more cautiously this time, his fists cocked. And Charlie Two-Moon let him come, then his left hand pumped out like a piston and hit Teeter flush on the mouth, rocking him back. Charlie came in with his right hand then, making it a good one, using his wiry strength behind it, and Teeter spun under the force of the blow, banged into the counter, bounced again, and fell without moving.

Jim Holbrook opened his knife again and went back to paring his nails. "That didn't last long, did it?" He asked the question of no one in particular and they all looked at him. He raised an eyebrow to Mel Allen. "Well, help him, damn it. He's your friend, ain't he?"

"Yeah," Mel Allen said and bent down to Fred Teeter. He half lifted him to a sitting position and moved his head from side to side. "Fred. Fred, wake up." He looked up appealingly. "Maybe we ought to throw some water on him, do you suppose?"

"Suit yourself," Holbrook said. He stepped

away from the counter and went out of the store. Pete Scarbrough got up and came around to his side and stood there, waiting to take Charlie Two-Moon's order.

5

Jim Holbrook leaned against the wall of the harness maker's place and waited, and when he saw George Grant hurrying down the street, he stepped away from the building and blocked Grant's path.

The constable was a heavy man with considerable stomach hanging over his belt and he looked at Holbrook with some annoyance.

"Get out of my way," he said.

"I'm trying to save you some trouble," Holbrook said softly. "Teeter and Mel Allen were going to have some fun. It backfired in Teeter's face." He looked at Grant steadily. "I'd tell that to the judge, George, providing anyone was foolish enough to arrest Charlie Two-Moon for this."

Some of the annoyance left Grant's round face. "That ain't the way Mel told it to me."

"Mel's a liar," Holbrook said flatly.

George Grant scratched the back of his head. "Well, no complaint has been signed. It might pay to let this go." He started to turn, then stopped. "Jim, I never knew you to mix in another man's quarrels. Besides, I thought you and Teeter were

55

good friends. You've played poker with him for years."

"I'll play with any man I can win regularly off of," Holbrook said, then smiled. "Teeter's been paying my grocery bill for three years now. Friends?" He shook his head. "I pick 'em closer than that."

"I sure don't figure you, Jim," Grant said. "Takin' up for an Indian."

"Maybe you're figuring it backwards," Holbrook said.

"How's that?"

"I might take up with the devil himself if he was against Fred Teeter."

This puzzled George Grant. "Be damned if I can figure what he's done to you."

"Does it have to be to me?" Holbrook asked. He turned and went back to Scarbrough's and saw the boxes on the counter. Charlie Two-Moon was lifting one, getting ready to carry it outside, and Holbrook said, "I'll give you a hand."

"Thanks," Charlie said and led the way to his wagon in the alley. They put the boxes in back and then Charlie said, "You turned off pretty clumsy in there, tripping Mel Allen that way."

"Sometimes I'm all thumbs," Holbrook said casually. Then he looked at Charlie and laughed. "Teeter thought you'd be easy. Now I never would have made that mistake."

"No, you wouldn't have," Charlie said. "Fact

is, I can't recall you ever making many mistakes, Jim."

"I've made 'em," Holbrook admitted. "A few I still regret." Then he laughed and took out his sack of tobacco and offered it. "I was about to ride on home. If you don't mind, I can tie my horse behind the wagon and ride a mile with you."

"Company's welcome," Charlie Two-Moon said. He smoked his cigarette and waited while Jim Holbrook went for his horse, and he thought about the man, remembering him from school days; Holbrook had been in the class ahead, a quiet, serious young man whom no one seemed really to know. Pieces of memory came back, and he recalled that Holbrook had been considered girl-shy, which probably accounted for his remaining a bachelor.

Holbrook returned with his horse, tied him to the tailgate, then got on the seat beside Charlie Two-Moon and they drove out of town.

"I've been thinking about riding over to your place," Holbrook said, "but I hate to butt in on a man uninvited."

"You're invited," Charlie said. "And if you need any help, send up smoke."

This allusion to his Indian blood surprised Jim Holbrook for he would never have said it, then he looked at Charlie Two-Moon and found him smiling.

Holbrook laughed then and said, "I guess I understand you, Charlie. Can you consider sack tobacco a peace pipe?"

"Done," Charlie said and took the Durham and held the reins between his knees while he rolled.

"George Grant wanted to know why I turned on Teeter in the store," Holbrook said. "Damned if I could tell him."

"Couldn't, or wouldn't?" Charlie asked.

"Wouldn't," Jim Holbrook said. "Some business a man's just got to keep to himself."

At the turnoff to Holbrook's place, Charlie stopped the wagon and Holbrook untied his horse and mounted up. He waved and rode off and Charlie went on for a mile, and when he came to his own road, he kept straight, driving toward the reservation.

He arrived in the early evening and his breath was frosty when he tied up by agency headquarters. Jules Kerrick came out and said, "You didn't take long to make up your mind."

"I told you I wouldn't," Charlie said. "I've got two boxes of stuff in the wagon."

"We'd better lock it up tonight or it'll be gone in the morning."

He went with Charlie to put up the team and they locked the wagon in the barn and on the way back to headquarters Charlie looked again at the place where he had been raised. Agency land was poor land and the houses the government had built for the Indians were shacks, old now, filthy with lice, for the Indians never wanted them in the first place and could not be taught to clean them. The place had a stink of its own, part stockyard and part litter left by two generations of living in squalor.

"The day I left this place to live in town," Charlie said, "Doc Carney shaved my head and gave me a bath in kerosene to get rid of the lice. Then he burned my clothes. He was kind about it, but a fourteen-year-old boy can still be humiliated because he's lousy."

"Charlie, wasn't there anything good here for you? Wasn't there family love?"

"Yes," he said. "But it takes more than that, Jules. A boy has to be taught about the world. I mean the world outside the boundary of this reservation. They've got to stop closing themselves off in their minds, Jules. When a woman has a baby she's got to go to the doctor, not have it squeezed out of her with a strip of blanket tied around her belly. Jules, when I was ten, my mother took me to town. All the stores had back rooms then where they waited on the Indian trade, but this time the clerk let us come into the main part of the store. I really thought that was something, until he showed my mother a cake of red soap. I'll never forget it because it had flowers molded into it, and my mother tried to eat it while everyone stood around and laughed. She didn't understand English or speak it and she got mad when I took the soap away from her. When we got back to the reservation, my father beat me for disgracing her in front of people."

"You must have thought there was damned little justice in the world," Kerrick said.

Charlie Two-Moon looked at him. "Is there?"

"Sometimes I've wondered myself," he admitted and they went inside.

Kerrick's quarters were in the rear of the building and Edith seemed pleasantly surprised to see Charlie Two-Moon. "I heard someone outside," she said. "You're in time for supper. I'll make up the spare room." She glanced at her husband, her eyes sparkling. "I think I'll invite another guest for supper."

She went back to the kitchen, humming softly to herself, and Jules Kerrick motioned for Charlie to sit down and offered a cigar. "I'm glad you decided the way I suggested," Kerrick said. "It's better."

"Let's hope so." He puffed on his cigar a moment, then said, "I may have to stay a day or two, Jules. Indian protocol, you know. And I won't be able to rush these negotiations."

"I understand," Kerrick said. "You're my guest as long as you like."

Edith came out of the kitchen. "Jules, watch the potatoes. I don't want them to boil over. I'll be back in a minute." She went out before he could say anything.

"If you were planning on company—" Charlie began.

"No, no, just someone Edith wants to invite. A teacher here. Lives in the building. Kind of new here. Only been here two years." He rolled the cigar around in his mouth. "Don't look stricken, Charlie. You're a man of the world who can hold up his end of a conversation."

"I could use a white shirt and a tie," Charlie said. "That's what I was thinking about."

"Hell, use one of mine," Kerrick said, getting up. He motioned for Charlie to follow him and they went into the bedroom and he got a shirt out of the drawer. Charlie put it on, surprised at how well it fitted, then he knotted the tie, and they started back to the living room just as Edith came in, laughing at something that had been said.

She was standing so that she partially blocked Charlie Two-Moon's view, then she stepped aside and he got a look at the Kerricks' guest.

"Charlie, this is Martha Frank. Charlie Two-Moon."

He walked up to her mechanically and they shook hands and her palm was warm and firm and he looked into her eyes and found them gray and frankly appraising. She was Indian, or part Indian for her color was golden and her hair was a dark, rich brown and she had the

61

cheekbones, not prominent, but still Indian.

Martha Frank smiled and said, "Three generations ago my great-grandmother was taken by Comanches and had a child. Now and then the blood crops up."

"Well hooray for the side of the Indians," Charlie Two-Moon said, smiling widely.

Edith looked shocked and Jules Kerrick seemed to hold his breath, then Martha Frank laughed explosively and put her hand up to her mouth. She said, "Charlie, you're the first person I ever told that to who didn't say how sorry they were. I'm going to like you."

"Maybe I could get you to help me with my arithmetic?"

"All right now," Jules said jokingly. "Let's keep it honest." He glanced at Martha Frank. "Charles graduated from high school, A number one in his class. Straight A's."

"It wasn't that I was smart," Charlie said. "I just sat next to a girl who never learned to cover her paper."

"I've got to see to supper," Edith said.

Martha Frank said, "Let me help you."

"Well, if you insist. But wouldn't you rather visit?"

"I'd hoped there was an alternative," Martha Frank said.

"I think I'll help my wife," Kerrick said, then quickly held up his hands. "No expressions of gratitude or shocked surprise, dear." He marched by her with a most pious expression on his face.

When they were alone and sitting down, Charlie said, "This has all the earmarks of a cooked-up deal. I hope it doesn't embarrass you."

"It doesn't," she said, "because I've heard a lot about you, Charlie. Some of my children talk about you and the time you came home from the war bearing honorable wounds and a very important medal on your chest."

"That was all a mistake," Charlie said, smiling. "You see, it was dark and I got mixed up in my directions, so when I ran, it was toward the Germans instead of my own trench. Afterward, it was too complicated to explain."

"Now that's all an interesting lie," Martha Frank said. "I know the truth. So does every child over six on the reservation. You're their hero, Charlie Two-Moon and every day I hear someone say 'When I get older, I will leave this place and be a big man like Charlie Two-Moon.' "

His manner turned serious. "Now you're not stretching that a little, are you?"

She shook her head. "There are more ways than one to explore, Charlie. There is more than land and mountains and oceans to conquer."

"Yes," he said softly. "That's certainly true."

"Come see us here, Charlie. There's good to be done here. Good that only you can really do." She reached out and took his hands and turned

63

them palms up so the roughness, the marks of hard work showed. "Touch them with your hands, Charlie. Let them feel the hands that soldiered for six years in order to earn the money to buy your farm. You know them, understand them and how much faith they put in their medicine. Then give them the medicine of your hands. Give them some of the faith you have."

Her words got to him, reached down in him and touched his wishes and his regrets. He said, "You must be a great teacher."

"No, I don't think so," she said. "I came here because it was a retreat. That's not a good reason."

"Things change," he said. "Sometimes we start out one way and end up another. We find the good reasons as we go along." He realized that he was holding her hands, and gently let them go. "Maybe you could find the time to come and visit me, you know, if the Kerricks were coming over."

"Is it only with that stipulation?"

"Oh, no," he said quickly. "I was just trying to—"

"I know what you were trying to do," she said. "You're a considerate man, Charlie."

Edith Kerrick came to the doorway. "It's on the table."

They got up and Charlie Two-Moon offered her his arm and she took it and they went into the dining room where he helped her with her chair then went around the table to his place across from her.

He looked at the roast and mashed potatoes and green peas and said, "Now this does beat my cooking by far."

Kerrick said grace, then began passing dishes around and it was some minutes before the activity subsided and they began eating.

"Martha is a Vassar girl," Kerrick said.

Charlie smiled. "I'm impressed. But I was before you told me."

"Charlie was also in a fist fight this afternoon," Kerrick said.

They all looked up, and color came to Charlie Two-Moon's face. "Aw, did you have to say that? And how did you know?"

"I have a telephone," Kerrick said. "Doctor Carney called me. I meant to congratulate you earlier but it slipped my mind." He glanced at his wife. "Fred Teeter felt brave in the hardware store."

"Him," Martha Frank said disgustedly. "I have two of his children in my class." She looked at Charlie Two-Moon frankly. "Yes, I'm afraid there are some men in town who'd be afraid to throw a rock in the school yard for fear of hitting some of their own."

"Next time," Charlie said softly, "I'll hit him a little harder."

"From what Doc Carney tells me," Kerrick said, "his head will ache for a week as it is. Edith, would you pass the gravy? Thank you, dear." He glanced at Charlie Two-Moon. "Teeter says he's going to kill you. Just talk, of course. Men don't do things like that anymore."

"When did they stop?" Charlie asked, and when he got no answer, he went on eating.

6

The next morning, Charlie Two-Moon drove his wagon to the house of Ed Lame Bear. Word had already gone out that he was on the reservation with a wagon and Tom Walks Far was there, with his wife and children and all her relatives; there were thirty people in Ed Lame Bear's small shack, and more were gathering.

Ed Lame Bear came up to the wagon, wearing the air of a man badly abused. He wore an old, much-patched coat, and a shapeless hat, and Charlie Two-Moon knew this was an act; the old man had put on his worst rags to portray his abject poverty. Some of the smaller children had been stripped naked so that Charlie Two-Moon could see how poor they were.

He felt like telling Ed Lame Bear to get their clothes on, that he intended to give them the gifts anyway, but he could not do this for the old man would lose face, be insulted, and take nothing, and the breach would be widened, possibly so far that it could never be bridged again.

"We will carry the things inside so they will be safe," Ed Lame Bear said, motioning for men to unload the wagon. "You will want to walk around and visit friends. It is right that you do this and it will give my lazy wife time to clean my house, so it will disgrace me less."

This too was part of the game. Ed Lame Bear and his kin wanted time to go through the boxes and pick what they wanted so they could bargain more sharply when the time came. And as for cleaning the house, Charlie knew that a little dirt would be thrown over the dung in the corners and that would be all.

"I had wanted to visit," Charlie said. "If I get done, I may return this afternoon."

He left his team and wagon, knowing they would be safe, for while they were parked outside Ed Lame Bear's door they would not be touched.

There was no order to the shacks; once they had been in neat rows, but they had been moved many times and were now scattered over many acres. The Indians ranched the land, raising pigs and sheep and goats and few cattle.

He had not left the vicinity of Ed Lame Bear's place when he found a parade of children following him and he was sorry he had no candy to give them. Still that would have been bad, for it would have made even worse beggars of them.

They knew him here, and when he stopped, they gave him polite respect for he was of them and a man apart from them and at the same time a man who had come back yet had not come back at all. The children followed him about all morning, keeping a respectable distance, but following him just the same.

Charlie Two-Moon talked to many people, and at the shack of Juan Teel, a young man came to the door. Charlie said, "I would speak to your father, if I may."

"He is dead," the boy said. "I'm his oldest son, Joe."

Charlie Two-Moon immediately noticed that the boy did not speak schoolbook English; he used contractions of words and no idiom at all. "Then since you're the man of the house," Charlie said, "I'll talk to you."

"I kept hoping you'd stop," Joe Teel said. He was, Charlie guessed, fourteen, and big for his age. From the light color, he supposed he was Pawnee, for he had the cheekbones and the solid shoulders so common among them. "You don't remember me, Charlie Two-Moon, because I was one of them—" He pointed to the children grouped in the yard "—and followed you about the last time you were here. You wore your uniform and the medal then. Why aren't you wearing it now?"

"I'm not a soldier now," Charlie said. "Are you alone here, Joe?"

He nodded. "Someday I'll leave, Charlie Two-Moon. I've saved my money and have eight dollars."

"What do you want to buy with eight dollars, Joe?"

"Books so I can go to high school in town," Joe Teel said. "Miss Frank tells me I should do this because my marks were good in the reservation school."

"It's a pretty tough world out there," Charlie Two-Moon said. "Where would you live?"

Joe Teel shook his head. "I don't know. I thought maybe you could tell me, Charlie Two-Moon."

"Me? Why did you think that?"

"Because you've been away to far places and fought in the war. They say you know many things, even more than the medicine man, although I no longer think he knows anything." He ducked inside and came back with a book, Dickens' *Tale of Two Cities*. "I've read this five times, Charlie Two-Moon, and there is more in this book than the medicine man will ever know. Have you read it?"

"Yes. Do you like to read, Joe?"

The boy nodded. "Books are very hard to get though. Miss Frank says they sometimes cost a dollar apiece. It's a great deal of money."

"Maybe I could talk to Miss Frank and see if she has any more she could spare."

Joe Teel raised his head high. "She has already offered me books but I can't take gifts when I haven't anything to give in return."

"Now you're thinking like a stupid Indian," Charlie said flatly.

The insult hit Joe Teel, hurt him, stunned him, and he stood there, torn between letting out his hot reply and holding it back in respect for this man who was a hero to him. "What would you say if I offered you a book?" He waited, knowing that Joe Teel wouldn't answer. Then he said, "Save your money, boy," and walked away.

It was time to go back to Ed Lame Bear's shack and he dreaded it, but it had to be done. He was met at the door and taken inside. A blanket had been thrown on the floor and Tom Walks Far was there, and three others, all distant relatives of Charlie Two-Moon.

"We are humbled, thinking of the many things you must have in the boxes," Ed Lame Bear said.

"Nothing I have is good enough for you," Charlie Two-Moon said. He looked at Tom Walks Far and was pleased to see the discoloration on his face, yet he let none of this show in the expression of his eyes.

"I have not slept well since there was anger between us," Ed Lame Bear said. "At first I thought it was the cold that kept me from sleeping, then I found that it was the trouble in my mind."

So he wanted a blanket or two, Charlie thought. He said, "It is getting cold out. Because I too have been thinking about you, I bought some blankets. They are thin and cheap and you will need at least two to keep your shoulders warm, but they are yours if you wish to accept them."

Ed Lame Bear protested strongly that this was too much, but he took the blankets and a third because Charlie Two-Moon insisted they were very thin.

He spent the rest of the day there and this polite trading went on and by the time he left, by the time the boxes were empty, everyone's pride had been soothed, and even Tom Walks Far's bruises had been healed.

Charlie did not want to stay and eat with them, and getting out of it was a delicate matter; he managed it by saying that he had promised the Kerricks and to back out now would be dishonorable.

They understood that and he left and drove back to headquarters. He put up the team and walked toward the porch and saw Joe Teel come out, two books under his arm. Martha Frank was with him and when Charlie Two-Moon came up, Joe Teel said, "Today you have shown me that I am not a man. But I'll give much thought to this, Charlie Two-Moon, so that the next time we meet you'll be proud of me."

He walked away then and Martha Frank said, "Just what did you say to that boy, Charlie?"

"Something stupid, I suppose. He's got to learn that it's not only wanting, but getting that matters." He knew this explanation wasn't going to satisfy her, still he hoped she wouldn't push for more. It was a feeble hope.

She shivered and crossed her arms. "Let's go inside before I freeze to death." She went in and walked ahead of him down the hall, then opened the door to her rooms. He hesitated, then thought better of it. "Coffee?"

"Yes, thanks." He went with her into the kitchen and took the cup she offered.

"I had Joe Teel for one year, his last in the reservation school," Martha Frank said. "He's a smart boy, and he's well ahead of the others because he goes ahead on his own and works. I gave him a mathematics book the first week I had him. At the end of the month he handed it back with all the problems worked. That boy should go to high school, Charlie."

"I guess he should."

Martha Frank waited and he waited and finally she said, "Well?"

"Well what?"

"Help him, Charlie."

"Give him money?"

"Don't be a damned fool," she said sharply. "Take him back with you, Charlie. Give him a home and his meals and let him go to school."

He frowned. "That's a pretty big step, isn't it?"

"You tell me that it is," Martha Frank said. She

stood there for a minute, observing him, then said, "All right, Charlie, then do the boy a favor. Go to him and tell him that you're really not a hero at all. Tell him the truth, that you got away because you couldn't stand people looking down on you because you were an Indian. But don't stop there, Charlie. Tell him all of it. Tell him that you hate Indians as much as any white man does."

He looked at her, not angry, not even hurt. "How do you know these things, Martha?"

"Because I was once like that," she said softly. "How do you think it was, growing up in Texas, both parents white as you'd want, and three brothers and a sister white and me with my damned olive skin and dark hair? Yes, I got out. I wanted to be so good, so big that people wouldn't dare to even think I was even part Indian. But they'd think it. It took a long time to realize that, Charlie. It's not good to be a prisoner, especially when you're a prisoner of yourself." She reached out and took him by the upper arms. "Take this boy, Charlie. Now, tonight."

"You want me to make a decision just like that?" He snapped his fingers. "Martha, I've worked hard and long to make my life the way I wanted it. Now you want me to change it, rearrange it so that Joe Teel can get off the reservation?"

"Yes, that's what I'm asking. It's a lot, isn't it?

In a way it's almost like asking you to die for what I want." She turned away from him. "Even now I wonder how I could ask it. I suppose it's because I have an almost blind faith in you, Charlie. I must have had it all along, just hearing about you and the things you've done." She looked back at him. "Charlie, some men just have to be messiahs. They can't help themselves. Why were you made strong? To use it selfishly?" She shook her head. "I'm twenty-six years old, Charlie, and I've never loved a man because I never saw what I thought a man should be. It isn't enough that he be young and handsome or have money and honesty and virtue. The man I could love must have destiny, Charlie. We all must have it in little ways or we're nothing but people crowding one another."

"What are you trying to say, Martha? That I could love you?"

She nodded. "Yes, I'm saying that, Charlie. Does it surprise you? I don't really think so, for you see we always know each other longer than the clock or the calendar shows. We carry ideals around in our heads and we keep matching up those ideals with the people we meet and hoping the pieces will all fit." She reached out and took the cup from his hand. "Your coffee's cold; let me warm it."

He smiled gently. "Getting into deep water, Martha?"

"Yes," she said. "I may be making a fool of myself."

"Not that," he said. Then he stepped over to the stove and cupped her chin in his hand and turned her face toward him and up to him and gently kissed her. She stood motionless, like a fawn ready for flight; he swore she did not even breathe, and when he pulled back she smiled and opened her eyes.

"What a woman you are," he said softly. "I can see now that men would be afraid of you because you're strong."

"Are you afraid of me?"

He shook his head. "No, not afraid. We fear the things we think will hurt us, and you wouldn't do that. But you could put a man in your hand, Martha, and you could mold him."

She studied his face, then reached up and touched his cheek. "There's strength in your face, Charlie, and in your eyes."

He laughed. "You know what I think? I think that when I leave here I'll go over to Joe Teel's shanty and take him back with me."

"Because I've made you do this?"

His smile remained. "Well, let's say that if I do it, it'll be because you had a large part in it."

"If you did that, Charlie, it would be because you really wanted to and not because of what I said."

He shrugged. "I kicked the boy in his false pride today. Now you never thought for a minute I was too big to take some of the same medicine, did you?"

"No."

"Then again I may show you some of this strength you say I have and go on home and let Joe Teel live his own life." He raised his coffee cup and sipped, being careful not to burn his lips. "I've got to think about this, Martha."

"How long?"

He let the silence run for a minute. "Well, if I don't hurry, I might have time to eat a piece of pie or something."

"Charlie, I'm serious."

"So was I," he said. Then he laughed and put his arms lightly around her. "I don't know what Doc Carney was thinking years ago, but he probably had plenty of doubts. Right now I can think of more reasons for going on home alone than for taking Joe Teel with me. But you're right, Martha; I've got to reach back whether I want to or not." He dropped his arms away. "Maybe I could get you to talk Jules Kerrick into heating some water for a boy's bath, and getting out the hair clippers?"

"I'd be glad to," she said. "I'll even give the dog a bath myself."

He frowned pleasantly. "What dog?"

"Well, he has a dog, a collie."

77

"Somehow you forgot to mention that," Charlie Two-Moon said. "Martha, I'm going to have to watch you a little closer."

"Why," she said, smiling, "that would be nice."

7

There was a lamp burning in Joe Teel's shack when Charlie Two-Moon approached the door; he knocked and the boy opened the door and stared in surprise.

"Come in, Charlie Two-Moon. The fire is small but it takes the chill from the air."

Stepping inside, Charlie Two-Moon looked around the small room; there was poverty here, but clean poverty. He said, "I've come to ask you if you'd like to live with me and go to school."

The boy seemed to hold his breath and he carefully put down the book he had been reading. "This isn't a joke you're playing on me?"

"Dead serious," Charlie Two-Moon said. "It's all right with Mr. Kerrick. You can go back with me tonight." He looked in the corner; the dog slept on a folded blanket, head on his paws. "The dog too."

Joe Teel sat down on his pole bunk. "I own only a few things. But I'm strong. I'll work for my food."

"You'll go to school and learn," Charlie said. "That comes first. You'll have chores. We all have chores in this world, but if I wanted a hired hand I'd have hired one. Get your things in a bundle."

"What of my sheep? How can I sell them?"

"Mr. Kerrick can take care of that for you," Charlie said. "Well, do you want to come with me or don't you?"

"It is such a big thing to make up one's mind so fast."

"That's the way it is with big things," Charlie said. "It's only the unimportant things where you have lots of time."

"I'll go," Joe Teel said, "because I feel that if I don't you'll never ask again. Is that right?"

"Yes."

The boy nodded and began to roll his blankets and extra clothes; he had very little and it was not a large bundle. His eight dollars was taken out of its hiding place, and he whistled and the dog heeled.

Before he opened the door, Joe Teel said, "Charlie Two-Moon, was this in your mind when you talked to me earlier?"

"No," he said honestly.

He thought about this and said, "I promise that you'll never be sorry you did this, Charlie Two-Moon."

"That's an odd thing to say, Joe."

"I think it's the truth. You no longer like your people, Charlie Two-Moon; I could see that today. I don't think you even like me because you're doing this for someone else, not for me. But it's like the rain that melts the mud of the walls and makes the grass grow at the same time; it's both good and bad, and it's up to me to make it a good thing, for you and for me."

"You're a wise boy," Charlie said and stepped outside.

Joe Teel left his home by turning his back on it and walking away, and it struck Charlie Two-Moon that he had done exactly the same thing once, but his feelings about it had been different from Joe Teel's.

At the reservation headquarters, Jules Kerrick and his wife met them and they went inside. Martha Frank was there, and Doctor Parker, who had to sign a certificate of health, stating that anyone leaving the reservation was not tubercular or had any other communicable disease.

Parker was a wisp of a man in his fifties and he had about him the flavors of a hot mince pie, and Charlie Two-Moon wondered, as he had for years, if Parker was ever completely sober. He signed the certificate and excused himself; he did not like people and made little pretense about it.

"I'll be the barber tonight," Jules Kerrick said and put his thumbs through the armholes of his vest.

Joe Teel looked at him, then at Charlie Two-Moon. "What is this?"

"You're going to get a haircut," Charlie said.

"You don't want the kids in school to make fun of you, do you?"

"I have no lice," Joe Teel said proudly. "Each week I scrub my cabin with strong soap and lye water. My dog has fleas, but—"

"I wear my hair short," Charlie Two-Moon said softly. "Is it enough that I ask this?"

"Yes," Joe Teel said.

"We'll wash the dog in my room," Martha said. "Has he ever had a bath, Joe?"

"Well, sometimes he will wade a creek. A bath, no."

"Then he's in for a new experience," Martha said. She whistled and the dog looked at her, ears alert, but he made no move to follow her. Charlie Two-Moon laughed softly and snapped his fingers and the dog came to him and sat by his feet.

"Male superiority," Martha said in mock disgust. "Isn't it sickening?"

In her quarters she had a large galvanized washtub sitting in the middle of the floor and Charlie lifted the dog in it after she had blended the water to the proper temperature. The collie didn't like this at all but was too mannerly to growl or snap, although he thought about it during the soaping and rinsing.

They dried him thoroughly and went back to Kerrick's rooms. Joe Teel looked like a different boy with his long hair properly cut and he kept raising his hand to the back of his neck to feel the short hair there.

Charlie Two-Moon got his wagon and brought it around front and the dog got in back while Joe Teel sat on the seat and waited for Charlie to mount up. Kerrick and his wife came out and Martha hugged the boy and said, "Keep the books, Joe. Never throw books away."

"I'll remember," he said.

"And I'll sell your sheep for you and bring you the money," Jules Kerrick promised.

"See that you are not cheated," Joe Teel advised. "Two ewes will lamb soon, but they will all try to make you think they are fat with bloat."

"I'm a pretty good horse trader myself," Kerrick said, and stepped back, and Charlie clucked to the team, turned the wagon and drove back toward his own place.

The hour was very late when they got to his farm and he lit the lamps and built a fire to take the chill off the air. He showed the boy the back bedroom, gave him blankets and a lamp for the room, then said, "The dog can sleep in here, but you get up and let him out when he scratches at the door. No piles on the floor, you understand?"

Joe Teel nodded and sat down on the bed and sank deep into it. "Feathers? I have never slept on such a bed."

"Then learn fast. Dawn comes around pretty quick."

He went out and into his own room and undressed and the feeling he had about this house was somehow diminished; he supposed it was because someone else lived here now. He was tired and yet not sleepy and he settled in bed and listened to the wind blow the tree branch against his roof and wondered if he had made a mistake.

Too late now, he told himself. Tomorrow he'd have to take the boy to town and register him at the school and to pay his tuition, and then he'd have to get him some clothes and he supposed there'd always be something every day he'd have to do for him, and he wondered if he could do this, think of someone else when he had spent all his life thinking of himself.

Horace Rector waited on Charlie Two-Moon; they had been classmates, not friends, not enemies, just classmates. Charlie bought Joe Teel some blue jeans and two corduroy shirts and a short coat and a stocking cap and a pair of shoes and overshoes and some heavy mittens, and the bill came to sixteen dollars.

As Rector wrapped the package containing Joe Teel's old clothes, he said, "The boy's going to school, eh?"

"Yes," Charlie said. Joe Teel was walking around the store, feeling the stiffness of his new jeans, listening to the squeak of his shoes.

"Do you think it's right, Charlie?" Rector asked.

"What's right?"

"Well, to let him go through what you went through?"

Charlie Two-Moon shrugged. "Horace, you wore glasses and had buckteeth. What did you go through?" He waited for the man to answer, and when he didn't, he asked, "Don't we all have something?"

"I never looked at it that way, Charlie," Rector said. Then he called Joe Teel over. "Come here, boy." He reached behind the counter and brought out a leather belt. "You wrap this around your schoolbooks and carry them over your shoulder. You see?"

"Yes," Joe Teel said. "How much does it cost?"

"It's a gift from me," Horace Rector said.

Joe Teel took it and said, "It's a fine belt, as good as the one I wear. Why do I deserve this gift?"

Horace Rector was taken back by the directness of the question, then he said, "Because I remember what it's like to wear glasses and have buckteeth."

Joe Teel looked at Charlie Two-Moon, a puzzled frown on his face. "Do you understand that, Charlie Two-Moon?"

"Yes. Mr. Rector is your friend."

The boy smiled then and so did Horace Rector,

and Joe Teel took the bundle and they left the store. They drove to the school and Charlie Two-Moon took him to the principal's office and the girl in the outer office asked them to wait a few minutes.

Then they went in, and Austin Mortenson came around the desk and shook hands. "How are you, Charlie?" Then he smiled at Joe Teel. "Who's this fine young man?"

"His name is Juan Teel, but he likes Joe better. I want to enroll him in high school. You'll find he's a good student."

"I see," Mortenson said and sat down. "Well, I think we can do that; the school board will certainly pass on it." He leaned back in his chair. "Right after you bought the farm from my brother, my wife and I had dinner at Milo's house and we talked about you. It rather surprised me, Charlie, that you came back here. After all, you've seen a good deal of the world and I rather thought you'd find someplace else more attractive."

"I didn't," Charlie said. "You came back here, didn't you?"

"Because I wanted to be a schoolteacher," Austin Mortenson said. "Just as Milo wanted to be a banker." Then he laughed. "I think I understand. You wanted to be a farmer."

"There," Charlie said, "you see how simple it all is." He crossed a leg and hooked an arm around the back of his chair. "Since I was a boy

I've looked at that farm, one of the finest pieces of land around here. I've seen one man after another go broke on it because he was careless or lazy or didn't know what he was doing, and I swore someday I'd have that place and make something of it. Don't we all have our dreams?"

"We'd be lost without them," Austin Mortenson said. Then he looked at Joe Teel. "What is your dream, son?"

"To stand tall like Charlie Two-Moon," Joe Teel said simply.

For a moment there was a deep silence in the office, then Austin Mortenson said, "I hope to live to hear someone say that of me." He drew a blank form to him and dipped his pen and asked the questions, and when it was filled out he signed it, then turned it so that Charlie Two-Moon could sign it. "I'll do my best on this with the school board, Charlie, but you know Fred Teeter. Whatever he does, Mel Allen will go along with. Pete Scarbrough is a neutral; there's no way to tell which way he'll swing. Dr. Carney is solidly on my side."

"The boy's got to go to school," Charlie said.

"Yes, I know. Someday they will all have to go to school. The trouble is, men like Teeter can't see that. Sometimes I don't think he can see much of anything." Then he shook his head and changed the subject. "You bought that farm at a bad time of the year, Charlie. You'll have to wait until next fall to bring in a crop."

"I have an idea or two," Charlie said. He unkinked his long legs and got up, putting his hand on Joe Teel's head. "Maybe you'd like to stay and have Mr. Mortenson show you around the school?"

Joe Teel nodded and Charlie Two-Moon understood how he felt, afraid because of the sudden newness, but it was a fear that would have to be surmounted, a fear that would have to be hidden, for if the boys saw it, discovered it, suspected it, Joe Teel's life would be pure hell.

"He'll be all right," Mortenson said. "After all, Charlie, I've had experience showing boys around the school."

Charlie Two-Moon understood and put on his coat. "I'll pick you up in an hour, Joe."

He drove to the depot and went into the telegrapher's office, spent some time composing his wire, then took it to the operator behind the wicket, who carefully counted the words. "Two dollars and sixteen cents for the wire and forty-nine dollars for the express money order." He looked at Charlie Two-Moon. "Rabbits?"

"Nice, fat, gray rabbits," Charlie said and paid him.

"Rabbits run wild on the prairie," the man said.

"Not this kind of rabbits." He buttoned his coat

88

and stepped outside. The sky was leaden and there was no hint of a warming sun. A stiff wind blew from the northeast and he reckoned the snow would arrive before dark. He was ready for it. His wood supply was laid in and he had the pantry full of food and the root cellar pretty well stocked, and all the outside work was finished.

It could blow up a good one for all he cared.

A man, he reasoned, had to do that with his life, button down all the loose ends and weather out the troubles that always seemed to come along. It was only when you didn't do that, didn't provide for the unexpected, that life stunned you, maybe even finished you off. It was Charlie Two-Moon's observation that bad trouble, when you could see it coming, never presented too much of a problem. He'd been in danger during the war, seen other men in danger, and had seen them survive it only to go under when there wasn't any danger at all. Life was what crushed a man, losing his job or his family, or his savings; those were the things that broke men.

He had some time to kill and walked up the main street and went into Al Winkler's barber-shop to get his hair cut. There was a customer in the chair and another waiting so Charlie took off his coat and hat and sat down. He looked out the front window and watched people walk up and down the street and Winkler's chair emptied and the man who'd been waiting moved into it and finally he got out and Charlie Two-Moon sat down.

Winkler snipped away and talked away and Charlie half listened. Then he saw Fred Teeter's wife leave the hotel with the two boys and walk toward the bank. He said, "Teeter comes to town at odd times, doesn't he?"

"Oh, I don't think he's in town," Winkler said. "Him and his wife don't live together anymore. She's been stayin' at the hotel and he's been livin' out at the place." He looked in the mirror at Charlie Two-Moon. "What do you make of it?"

"I don't make anything of it," Charlie said. "Should I?"

Winkler shrugged. "You know Fred; he's got to blame somebody."

"Me?" Charlie looked at him, then he laughed. "He's got the wrong pig by the ear this time."

"You ought to tell that to Fred then," Winkler said and shaved his neck.

8

Joe Teel rode one of Charlie Two-Moon's horses to school each day and left him in the stable, working an hour after school for the privilege. Once in a while he would take the team and wagon and bring back to the farm rolls of wire and lumber and hinges and anything else Charlie Two-Moon wanted, for Scarbrough always loaded the wagon and had it waiting for the boy to pick up after school.

The shipment of rabbits arrived and Charlie paired them in the hutches he had built inside the barn. A kerosene heater kept the temperature above freezing, and then it was a matter of feeding them and waiting.

His days were taken up with many chores. When snow fell, he had to shovel a path to the barn and the outhouse and the well, and he was always building more hutches. The barn was full of them, rows piled on rows with three elevated walkways to service them. Even the loft was filled. Then it came time to separate the bucks so the females could take care of the young, and he kept accurate records of mating and litters and feedings.

At night he would help Joe Teel with his

schoolwork. The boy was smart and worked hard, and if he had any problems in town, he left them there and never brought them home. He was a help around the farm, taking care of the evening dishes, and the problems Charlie had expected never came up, for Joe Teel could live Charlie's way, with none of the Indian habits that Charlie despised.

The weather remained mild and it snowed off and on for ten days, then the sun came out and the temperature plunged to ten below and the land was still, silent, blanketed, and Charlie knew it would stay that way for a while.

He did not leave his place for the rabbits required near-constant care, and only the trail leading to town, which Joe Teel took each day, marked any movement from the farm.

Then across the white, rolling land came a sleigh pulled by Jules Kerrick's team and Charlie saw it from the house and came out to help Martha Frank down.

"Mohammed comes to the mountain," she said and laughed, and sank to her knees in the snow. She had on a raccoon coat and a heavy scarf tied around her head and wool mittens. "Are you trying to be a hermit?" she asked.

"I've been busy," Charlie said.

She arched an eyebrow. "Shoveling snow?"

"Well, that too," Charlie said. "Come on in the barn. I'll show you my livestock."

He broke trail for her and she followed in his footsteps, stretching her legs to do so. The main door of the barn was sealed with burlap sacks and dirt had been banked high around the sides; they reached the path he kept shoveled and went in the small side door.

Immediately she could feel the warmth and then saw the large kerosene stove and the two barrels of fuel and the chimney running through the room, then she turned and stared at all the rabbit hutches.

"Why," she said, surprised, "I had no idea. How many rabbits do you have?"

"Well, I started out with thirty does and two bucks and after the first litters arrived, I had two hundred and eighteen. They've been bred again now."

"Charlie, whatever made you think of raising rabbits?" she asked.

"When I was in the army, I went on furlough with a fella. His father had raised them for years and I got interested. He sold me these. Told me he would when I was ready to start raising my own." He smiled. "Actually, these are not rabbits, but hares. There's a difference, you know."

"No, I didn't know."

"A true rabbit's young are born without hair and with their eyes closed. The hare's young have fur and their eyes open. These are Belgian hares and their fur is exceptionally fine and is quite valuable. Also the meat is a delicacy in the better city restaurants."

"But, Charlie, raising them in the wintertime—"

"It's the best time," he said. "In the summer, the price of rabbit meat is low. And in two months, the young are ready to market. Before Christmas I'll ship a hundred and fifty dressed rabbits at roughly eighty cents apiece. The furs will bring forty cents each. By March or April, when the market tapers off, I figure to have made eight hundred dollars, and set up my breeding hutches for next year. Of course I'll have to move them outside. Rabbits need sunlight." He pointed to the large skylights he'd put in the roof. "That's why I've got those there." He smiled. "Rabbits breed fast. A young rabbit is ready to breed in two and a half months, and they have from eight to twelve in the litter. You do a little mental figuring and it adds up fast. By next fall, say middle October, when the market is highest, I'll ship four thousand dressed rabbits."

"Why, that's almost five thousand dollars," Martha said, amazed. "There isn't a farmer in this whole country who'll net two thousand dollars' profit." She turned and looked again at all the rabbit hutches. "I'm surprised more people aren't raising them."

"It isn't quite as easy as it sounds," Charlie

said. "They've got to be fed right, good grains, a balanced diet, and they take a lot of care for they're susceptible to quite a few diseases. And they require constant attention. Each hutch must be cleaned every day and new straw put inside. I start at dawn, work through the day, and go back after supper until ten o'clock. Now you tell me how many farmers will put up with that? They'd rather put a sow and a litter in a pigpen and throw her some corn twice a day."

"You're right there," Martha said. "Are you going to plant a crop in the spring?"

"Yes, twenty acres of timothy. The rest of the land I'm going to let out on shares and let someone else work it. That area that was once the hog yard I think I'll chicken-wire fence and raise some turkeys."

"You're going to have everyone around here raising rabbits and turkeys," she said.

"Not much danger of it. Turkeys drive a lot of people crazy with their noise. And I don't know of anyone around here who'd put up with rabbits." He took her arm. "Come on in the house."

They went inside and he took her coat and hung it up and then started to make some coffee. She gently elbowed him aside. "Here, let me do that." He sat down at the table. "How is Joe doing in school?"

"Fine."

"No problems?"

"If there are, he hasn't brought them home."

She turned her head and looked at him. "How is it with you and the boy?"

"Just dandy," Charlie said.

She continued to look at him. "That's not really the answer I wanted to hear."

"What was it then?"

She shrugged. "Oh, I don't know. I suppose I wanted you to say that you were glad he's here. But I have no right to ask for all that. He *is* off the reservation and that's enough."

"Well, you'll say that but you don't really mean it."

"Mr. Kerrick sold Joe's sheep. I brought over the forty-two dollars."

"He'll like that," Charlie said.

The coffeepot began to thump and she took it off the stove. "I really should be starting back," she said. "It gets dark very early."

"Don't be in a rush," he said. "I haven't seen you in nearly two months."

"And whose fault is that?"

"Mine," he said. "A man shouldn't be that busy."

"I'm glad you realize that." She brought the cups to the table and sat down and he poured for them. "What time does Joe get home?"

He turned and looked at the alarm clock sitting atop the stove. "He should be coming along any

96

time." Then he smiled. "I thought you came to see me."

"You wouldn't want me to make that too obvious, would you?"

They drank coffee and then when her cup was half full, he topped it, and went to the stove to put in more wood. He looked out the kitchen window as Joe Teel rode into the yard and went to the horse shed.

"The boy's here," Charlie said, and went back to the table.

Joe Teel came in a few minutes later, looked at them in surprise, then turned quickly as they both got out of their chairs.

"Joe!" Martha said. "What's wrong with your face?"

He would have bolted for the bedroom if Charlie Two-Moon hadn't caught him by the arm and hauled him back. Blood splattered Joe Teel's coat and had dried on his cheeks and chin and it bubbled in his nose when he breathed.

"A fight?" Charlie asked.

"I didn't run," Joe Teel said.

"Now you sit right down here. Charlie, help him off with his clothes," Martha said. She got a pan and some hot water and the wash cloth and bathed his face. "Oh, dear," she said. "I think his nose is broken. Charlie, go to town for Doctor Carney."

"I'll be all right," Joe Teel said, but the warm

room was thawing him and pain was bothering him.

"You'll do as I say and get right to bed," Martha admonished. "Charlie, you go ahead. I'll stay here with him."

"It'll take me nearly two hours," he said.

"That doesn't matter." She gave him a small shove to get him going and he put on his coat and gloves and went outside to saddle the other horse.

Since the last snow the boy had worn a good trail to town and Charlie Two-Moon made as good time as he could without tiring the horse, and when he got to Carney's office he found that the doctor was not there and had to wait.

Thirty minutes later, Carney came in, looked not at all surprised, and said, "I wondered if he was hurt. He battered the hell out of Mel Allen's boy. Closed one eye and I had to take six stitches in his lip."

"To hell with Mel Allen's boy," Charlie said. "Where's your sleigh?"

"Outside. I have to eat once in a while you know," Carney said. "Don't I have time for supper first?"

"I'll feed you at my place," Charlie said. "Martha Frank's there with Joe."

Carney raised an eyebrow, but said nothing. He buttoned up his coat, picked up his bag and went ahead of Charlie Two-Moon down the stairs. Carney got in the sleigh and Charlie tied his horse behind and started to get in, but stopped when he saw Mel Allen hurrying down the street.

Carney said, "If you hit him, you'll only slow things up."

Allen came up. "I voted against that Indian kid in the first place."

"What were you ever for?" Charlie asked. "Get out of the way, Mel."

"By God, I'm going to sue!"

"Then see a lawyer," Charlie said and started to get into the rig. Mel Allen took hold of his coat and started to pull him back, but when Charlie whipped his head around and stared at him, Allen let go of the coat and stepped back.

As they drove out of town, Carney said, "He never does anything but talk."

"Because it's cheap," Charlie said.

"How bad's the boy hurt?" Carney asked.

"Martha thinks his nose is broken."

"We can fix that," Carney said. "The story I got is that there was some kind of a contest on at school and Joe beat Mel's kid out of first place. The fat went into the fire as soon as school let out." He looked at Charlie Two-Moon. "Mel's kid hit Joe just once. From then on it was, 'clean out the stable, Mother; the cows are coming home tonight.'"

"You're so funny," Charlie said, "you ought to be on radio."

"I rather have a flair for it," Carney said

and drove on with his aggravating indifference.

It was dark when they reached Charlie's farm and he led the way inside. Martha was in the kitchen and she took a lamp down the hall and put it on a small sideboard while Carney went on into Joe Teel's room.

Charlie poured some coffee and stood by the stove. "Mel Allen's boy," he said. "And Mel's mad about it."

"Joe told me," she said.

He looked at her, surprised. "He wouldn't have told me."

"Because he thinks you don't really care," Martha said. She stood with her arms crossed, bunching her breasts.

"But I do care," Charlie Two-Moon said. "All right, I didn't at first, but I like the boy here."

"Then tell him that. Show him."

"How?"

She shook her head. "You'll have to work it out for yourself, Charlie." She raised a hand and brushed her face. "Don't you want some supper?"

"I guess. The doc hasn't eaten."

"I'll fix it," she said and went into the pantry. She came back with potatoes and ham and canned tomatoes and some peaches, and began heating the skillet.

"Later," Charlie said, "I'll take you home."

"And who'll take care of your rabbits?"

He shrugged and didn't answer her.

She put down the potatoes she was peeling and came up to him. "I'll stay the night and go back in the morning. Now why don't you take care of your chores while supper cooks?"

"If it ever got out—"

"Why should I worry about that?" she said. "Charlie, I'm really not afraid of people."

"No, I guess not," he said and slipped into his coat. He took a lantern and went outside and was gone the better part of an hour. Then he came back, stamping snow off his overshoes before coming into the house.

Martha had the table set and Doctor Carney came out, polishing his glasses. "I've repaired the damage and given him something to make him sleep through the night." He looked at the table. "Food! Bless you, girl." He scraped back a chair and sat down. "Well come on, Charlie, let's lighten these groaning boards."

"Everything's ready," Martha said and they sat down; Carney was already cutting into the ham and heaping potatoes onto his plate.

"Truly a domestic scene," he said, glancing at Martha Frank. "And I won't ask why you're here."

"Well I can damned sure tell you," Charlie said hotly.

Carney held up his hand. "Peace, Happy Warrior. I have a blind faith in your continued virginity."

Martha smiled in a surprised way. "What's this?"

Charlie said, "Shut your mouth and eat, Doc."

"Words to live by," Carney said and ladled tomatoes into his dish.

9

Charlie Two-Moon came to town twice before the spring thaw, and each time he drove his wagon loaded with boxed, dressed rabbits; he shipped them to a St. Louis outlet and got his check in the return mail, and this he always deposited in Milo Mortenson's bank.

He could have cashed them, but in depositing them he was letting everyone know that this was profit and that he hadn't yet used up his ready cash. Mortenson, who liked a secured loan even more than a deposit, offered to loan money for expansion, but Charlie Two-Moon declined, preferring to pay cash as he went along.

Some things changed during the winter; Jules Kerrick had closed the reservation against visitors from town, unless cleared through him, and a deputy sheriff had arrested two men who had gone out there for a weekend away from their wives, which pretty well put a stop to that business.

A few babies had been born in town, and two older citizens had died, and the spring was coming and everyone was talking about that. Charlie had been looking forward to that part of the year, and before he went back to his farm he stopped at the telephone company and the electric light company.

And a few weeks later, right after the first thaw, a gang of workers came out to his place, erected poles, strung wires, and that night he turned a switch and lighted the place and put the lamps away, cleaned and filled, ready for emergency use. He had the telephone put in the kitchen, the walnut box mounted on the wall near the door, and Joe Teel thought this was wonderful, especially when Charlie called the reservation and talked to Martha Frank. He let Joe Teel talk to her also, and was pleased at the boy's excitement for he felt it himself.

Jim Holbrook came over several times and they worked out an arrangement to farm the land, with Holbrook buying the seed and taking the biggest percent of the crop. It was a good arrangement, fair to both, and gave Holbrook the advantage of having more land without the capital investment, and it gave Charlie the opportunity to make a profit, after taxes, on acreage that would have lain fallow.

Holbrook took his evening meal with Charlie Two-Moon and the boy, then got in his Ford truck and drove back to town. The road was slush and the chains banged against the rear fenders and he parked in front of the bank, then crossed over and went down the street to Mel Allen's pool hall.

Allen and Winkler were playing a game of

rotation; they looked up then went on with their game. Holbrook stopped by the cigar counter, reached in and took two Moonshine Crooks, and laid a nickel on the glass counter before going to the back where the tables were.

He sat down in one of the chairs along the side and said, "Seen Fred Teeter today?"

"No," Allen said, not looking up until he had made his shot. Then he walked around the table calking his cue. "You been out to the rabbit farmer's?" When Holbrook nodded, Allen said, "Are you going to farm his place?"

"We reached an agreement."

"I hope you stuck it to him good," Allen said. He made his shot then looked at Jim Holbrook. "What the hell are you doin' in town on Tuesday?"

"What does anyone do in town?" He lit his cigar and smoked it and now and then he got up and walked to the front of the pool hall and looked out at the street. Then he buttoned his coat and left, walked to the corner and crossed over. The main street was quiet, and only one store was lighted; he stopped in front of the bank, looked both ways, then went up the stairs to Doctor Oswald Carney's office. The door was locked and Holbrook tapped lightly and a moment later Carney turned the lock.

Carney said, "You took your time about getting here."

"I wanted to give Fred a chance," Holbrook said softly. "After all, he is her husband."

"Well, he hasn't showed up," Carney said. "I must have phoned him three hours ago."

Holbrook nodded. "When I heard his ring, I rubber-necked, then went over to Charlie Two-Moon's place. I've been in town a half hour." He licked his lips. "How is she, Doc?"

"She's started labor," Carney said. "Premature birth. We have to hope for the best. I don't hold much hope for the baby, to be honest with you. Premature is bad enough, but when the mother has had this type of disease—" He shook his head. "Jim, why don't you go over to the hotel with the boys. They're alone."

"All right," Holbrook said, turning to the door. "Doc, you'll let me know?"

"Of course," Carney said and showed him out, then locked the door behind him.

On the way down, Holbrook met Carney's nurse coming up, and she gave him a long, searching glance in passing, but did not speak. He stopped on the walk, then turned to the hotel and went into the lobby. Holbrook didn't have to ask the clerk her room number; he knew these things because he wanted to know them.

At the head of the stairs he turned right and walked along a short hall; these rooms were for permanent guests and they got a weekly or monthly rate, and for a single man it was cheaper than renting a house and hiring a housekeeper.

He knocked on a door and a boy of eight answered it. Holbrook said, "Hello, Buster. Can I come in?"

"Mama's not here."

"I came to see you and your brother," Holbrook said and stepped inside. He took off his hat and coat and laid them on a table, then sat down on the worn sofa. The boy looked at him, his eyes round and interested.

Then the boy said, "That's a funny-looking cigar. It's got a bend in it."

Holbrook laughed. "Called 'crooks.' Best two-for-a-nickel cigar on the market."

"Can you make smoke come out your ears?"

"No, I never tried that," Holbrook said. "I'm not much for tricks, but I know a story or two." He looked around. "Where's your brother?"

"Asleep. But I like stories."

"All right then, you just sit over here and I'll tell one to you, then you've got to go to bed." Holbrook patted a place beside him and the boy sat down and Holbrook began spinning a yarn out of his head, and he made it exciting enough for any boy. When his cigar was short and the story done, he got the boy off to bed, then went back to the other room and walked up and down, breaking cadence only now and then when he paused to listen for a step outside in the hall.

His watch stopped at eleven fifteen and he

cursed himself for forgetting to wind it, and later he heard Carney's step and had the door open before the doctor even got to the end of the hall. Carney came in, not saying anything, and stopped in the middle of the room.

Holbrook closed the door and said, "Well, dammit?"

"She's dead," Carney said. "Both dead. There's nothing to be done about it. Nothing I could have done to prevent it." He looked at Holbrook and found the man's complexion like chalk. "You'd better get a drink, Jim."

"I'm going to get a gun and kill a man," Holbrook said calmly. Carney, shocked, reached out to touch him, take hold of him, and Holbrook batted the hand aside and snatched up his coat and hat.

"Jim, don't be a fool!"

"He never even came to town," Holbrook said. "You'll call him, tell him I'm coming after him. Go ahead. I want him to know it."

"I'm going to call the constable too," Carney said. "Jim, you're losing your head." He took a step toward Jim Holbrook, who was at the door, then stopped when he saw the look in the man's eyes. "I can't stop you but there are men who will."

"Suit yourself," Holbrook said and stepped out.

Carney listened to the man run down the hall and waited; he had time and there was no sense in arousing the hotel. He took a dozen deep breaths, then calmly walked down the stairs to the lobby.

The clerk was not at the desk and Carney found him in a small room just off the lobby, catching up on his sleep; he shook him awake. "Get the constable and don't waste any time about it," Carney said.

"Wh—what's goin' on?"

"Get him!" The man stirred into motion and then Carney took him by the arm. "Do you keep a firearm behind the desk?"

"Yes, there's a .38 in the drawer."

"All right," Carney said and gave him a shove. "Get the constable."

The clerk ran out and Carney stepped behind the desk and opened all the drawers and found no .38 revolver there. "Smart guess," he said softly to himself. A Ford truck went down the street, hurrying out of town and Carney knew that would be Jim Holbrook; he turned to the wall phone and rang for the operator and silently cursed her when she took so long to respond.

"Get me Fred Teeter's farm," he said and stood there, drumming his fingers while the ringing went on.

Fred Teeter thought it was a dream at first, then got out of bed and stumbled through the dark house to answer his telephone. The floor was cold and he shivered in his underwear and jerked the receiver off the hook.

"Yeah? What the hell's the idea callin' me at this hour?" He shouted into the mouthpiece, then he pulled in his breath sharply and held it while Carney talked, and when Teeter spoke, his voice was hushed. "What's he want to do that for? By God, I'll kill him if he comes here." He clapped the receiver on the hook and stood there in the darkness a moment before going to his bedroom to dress.

Teeter didn't light the lamps; he thought about it and decided not to. It would be better if he waited in darkness. By God, he'd blow his stupid head off; this thought prompted him to go to the closet and load his shotgun and with this in his hands he felt more comfortable.

He went into the parlor to sit, where he could watch the road, and he kept telling himself that he wasn't afraid of Jim Holbrook. It put Teeter into a rage to think that another man had loved his wife, and there was no doubt in his own mind that Holbrook had been up to some sneaky business all along. It even occurred to Teeter then that maybe he hadn't picked up anything at all at the reservation, but instead had gotten his dose from his own wife, who'd got it from Jim Holbrook.

I'll enjoy killing him, Teeter thought, and waited for the first glimmer of headlights coming down his road.

He waited an hour and heard nothing, saw nothing, and he began to think that Holbrook had changed his mind.

Lost his nerve, that's what.

The house was very cold and he wanted to light the fire, but that would mean taking his attention off the road and he didn't want to risk that. The house felt drafty and he had never heard it so silent.

A board creaked in the floor; he knew the location of that board, in the hallway arch right behind him, and only a man's weight would make it creak.

Jim Holbrook said, "Goodbye, Teeter."

He screamed and leaped aside, whirling, letting go with both barrels of the shotgun, one right after the other, hearing the shot tear into the plaster and smelling the dust it raised before he ran to the window, plunged through, taking glass and frame with him.

Teeter landed in a snowbank, rolled and ran to the barn, still clutching his empty shotgun. He slammed open the doors, and hurriedly choked and cranked his car into life, then tore out of the yard, sliding and skidding the back wheels.

His road joined the town road three hundred yards past a small wooden bridge, and his headlights picked it up and he went over it, then his foot tramped heavily on the brake for he could see Jim Holbrook standing by the front fender of his Ford Truck, the revolver in his hand.

Teeter thought of ramming him, of shooting his shotgun, but instead of these things he swerved his car, took the ditch, and drove on down the road toward Charlie Two-Moon's place. Behind him, Jim Holbrook started his truck and the headlights went on and Teeter drove the Dodge wide open, feeling a prickle of fear at the base of his neck.

His shotgun was empty, and foolishly he had brought along no shells. He was sorry he hadn't rammed the Ford, but he had lost his nerve at the last moment, as Holbrook had figured he would and had been forced to turn this way.

He drove faster than he had ever driven before and still he could not shake Jim Holbrook's headlights, and when Teeter came to Charlie Two-Moon's gate, he nearly lost control of the car and crunched the rear fender against the post.

Stopping near the house, Teeter ran to the door and began to pound on it and when he got no instant response he began to beat on the lock with the butt of his shotgun. Then lights came on and Charlie Two-Moon flung the door open and Teeter bowled past him.

"You've got to stop him!" Teeter yelled. "Get your gun!"

"My gun has been in the bottom of a trunk

since the war," Charlie said calmly. "I'm not sure I have any shells for it."

"Oh, God!" Teeter said and looked as though he was going to fall.

"Who's after you?" Charlie asked, then looked out as the truck pulled into the yard. He glanced at Teeter. "Jim Holbrook's after you?"

Fred Teeter threw the empty shotgun halfway across the room as Holbrook came across the porch and stopped in the doorway. Then he stepped inside and closed the door.

"Charlie, this isn't your business," Holbrook said.

"My house, my business," Charlie said. "Put up the gun, Jim."

"Why, I haven't even used it yet," Holbrook said. He looked at Fred Teeter and his eyes were hard and expressionless. "She's dead and the baby's dead and no one is going to punish you at all, Fred. That's a bad thing, you know that? If a man steals, they put him in jail, but you, Fred, they'll do nothing to. That's not right."

Charlie Two-Moon said, "Jim, the biggest mistake you'll ever make in your life is to pull that trigger."

"No, I made my big mistake years ago when I kept my mouth shut and let Fred Teeter move in with his line of bullshit and talk her into marrying him." He never stopped watching Teeter. "You're shaking, Fred. The house too cold for you? Build

113

up a fire, Charlie. I want it warm in here. He'll shake anyway because his guts are jelly."

"Jim, I'm going to have to jump you," Charlie said calmly.

"And I'd have to shoot you," Holbrook said.

"Just to get at him? The shot will wake the boy. Will you kill him too?"

Holbrook's cheeks lost their granite hardness and he looked at Charlie Two-Moon, the appeal in his eyes. "What am I going to do then?"

"You're going to let him go. You're going to let him walk the streets and know that he's dirt. Tonight, all the people in the world have turned away from him, Jim. Don't you think that's enough?" He waited for Holbrook to say something, to answer, and when he didn't, Charlie Two-Moon reached out and gently took the .38 out of his relaxed hand.

Then the sheriff and two deputies came down the road.

10

Oswald Carney was the first man into Charlie Two-Moon's house, and he was closely followed by Ray Andrews and the two deputies; they stopped just inside the door and looked from one man to the other. Fred Teeter was leaning against the wall, his head turned away, forehead touching the molding around the kitchen entrance. Charlie held the .38 by the barrel as though he had no use for it and was looking for a place to put it. Jim Holbrook stood there, waiting, beaten, and yet victorious.

"Thank God no one got killed," Carney said. "We stopped at Teeter's place. From the buckshot holes we thought—"

"I'll take that pistol," Ray Andrews said. He was an arid-mannered man who didn't often get into this part of the county except on election years or when something like this happened. Charlie handed him the gun and Andrews put it in his overcoat pocket. "Now suppose someone tell me what happened here?"

Fred Teeter stirred. He pointed to Jim Holbrook. "He tried to kill me."

"I never fired a shot," Holbrook said calmly.

"Teeter did. He emptied his shotgun at me at fifteen feet and missed with both barrels."

Andrews took the pistol from his pocket, swung out the cylinder, and dumped six unfired cartridges in his hand. "It hasn't been fired," he said. "You'll have to come along, both of you. We'll get this cleared up in the morning."

Fred Teeter was insulted. "Arrest me? My God, I was defending myself against this maniac!"

"We'll see," Andrews said dryly. He nodded to his two deputies. "Take 'em out to the car."

Holbrook turned willingly, but it looked as though Teeter was going to put up a fight, then he changed his mind and turned to the door. Before Holbrook went out, Charlie Two-Moon said, "I'll come in town tomorrow, Jim."

"Thanks," Holbrook said and went out.

After they had gone, Andrews took off his hat and sighed. "I expected worse, indeed I did. Did you take the gun away from him, Charlie?"

"He handed it to me," Charlie said.

Andrews nodded. "Well, that's something in his favor. He sure got touched off, didn't he?"

"He had his reasons," Carney said. "It wouldn't be so bad, but Jim blamed himself for everything. He loved her, you see. Loved her for years, even before she married Teeter. But his own shyness, his own feelings of insecurity held him back from ever saying so, or showing her. Now she's dead and he thinks it's his fault. If he'd spoken out, her

116

life would have been different. Her life wouldn't have ended." He shook his head. "Teeter's lucky he's not dead."

"I don't think Jim could have killed him," Charlie said. "Care for some coffee? Just take a minute to stoke the fire and slide the pot on."

Ray Andrews shrugged. "Sounds fine. Doc, if I can ride back in your car I'll send the boys on in with the prisoners."

"I'll take you back to the county seat," Carney volunteered.

They went in the kitchen and Charlie built up the fire and they sat around the table, smoking and talking quietly and waiting for the coffee to heat.

Finally Charlie asked, "What's going to happen to Jim, Sheriff?"

"Well, it depends on Fred Teeter. If he doesn't prefer charges, not much will come of it." He glanced at Carney. "He didn't even come in town, you say? You told him his wife was in labor?"

"That and a few other things too," Carney said. He slapped the table in disgust. "Why do these things have to happen?" He looked from Andrews to Charlie Two-Moon as though he expected them to have the answer. "Now that I think of it, I've never had much use for Teeter. It used to gripe my soul to see his wife waiting on the hotel porch while he played cards or—" He waved his hand, not wanting to say more.

The coffeepot began to rock and Charlie got up and set out three cups, then poured. He offered them cream and sugar, then sat down. "What about the two boys?"

"Yes, there's always someone to tell," Carney said. "Andrews, the court ought to do something about this." He looked at Charlie. "Those kids can't stay at the hotel, and I'll be damned if I can see them with their father. Charlie, if I went to the judge, and asked him to put them in temporary custody, would you keep them here on the farm?" He held up his hands before Charlie Two-Moon could object. "I'm asking this as a friend, Charlie. I'm imposing and not apologizing for it."

Andrews sat there, saying nothing, and Charlie sipped his coffee before speaking. "It seems odd, with Teeter hating me, that you'd want me to—" He shrugged. "Yes, I'll keep the boys here, if it works out that way."

Carney smiled. "Charlie, you always restore my faith in human nature." He finished his coffee and got up. "Ready to start back, Sheriff?"

Andrews nodded and stood up. He shook hands with Charlie Two-Moon, then went out to Doctor Carney's coupe and a moment later they drove away. Charlie waited until they reached the road, then he turned out the parlor lights, and the one in the kitchen and went down the hall to his room. He cracked the door to Joe Teel's room and found

118

the boy sleeping soundly; he had been unaware of it all, and it was just as well, Charlie thought, for deep trouble comes soon enough; there was no sense in waking up and looking for it.

The next morning he got up well before dawn, and before the sun was full up he had his hutches cleaned and the feeding over, and after breakfast he went into town with the boy, promising to pick him up after school was out.

Doctor Carney had planned to drive over to the county seat with Charlie Two-Moon, but an emergency kept him from going, so he loaned his car to Charlie and he drove over by himself.

Checking with Ray Andrews at the sheriff's office, Charlie learned that Holbrook's hearing was scheduled for ten o'clock, and bail would be set at that time. He was allowed to see Holbrook for a few minutes, then they had to go to the courthouse.

Since it was just across the square, Andrews walked over with Charlie Two-Moon. "Fred Teeter wouldn't sign a complaint," Andrews was saying. "He swore he would last night, but this morning he'd changed his mind. That's a break for Holbrook although the county prosecutor might want to press a display of deadly weapons charge against him."

"Teeter did a little shooting," Charlie said. "Or doesn't that count?"

"We'll talk to the prosecutor," Andrews said and led the way through the building's many hallways. He went in through a door with a large frosted glass panel in it and introduced Charlie to a young man with short hair and gold-rimmed glasses.

"Why, I know you," Paul Sessler said. "You were a class ahead of me in school."

"Of course," Charlie said. "Your folks moved to Omaha right after your sophomore year." He shook hands and felt warmed that this man was happy to see him.

"Charlie would like to talk to you about this Teeter-Holbrook business that happened up-county last night. There seems to be no damage done, and Teeter wants to drop it," Andrews said. "Of course, if the docket of the justice court is running a little dry—"

Paul Sessler laughed. "Anything but that. I think we can move to release both parties here. But I got a telephone call from Doctor Carney earlier, concerning two minor, male children. Carney asked that this office recommend temporary custody of them in your favor, Charlie. I suppose you've given your consent?"

"Yes," Charlie said.

"This isn't a simple matter," Sessler said. "For the time being, a temporary order can be issued and a full investigation of this matter be instigated. But it's doubtful that anyone would deny the natural father his children, regardless of his questionable character. You see, the law's pretty firm on these points and—"

"Let's not go into that," Andrews said. "Just get me a release and a temporary custody order; my civil deputy can serve them in due time."

Sessler nodded and made a few notes on a pad of paper. "There's one thing I want you to clearly understand, Charlie. In the event that this office, in the course of investigation, proves to the court that Teeter cannot provide a suitable home, the children may be taken and made a permanent ward of the court, until such time that he remarries. In that event, the children would have to be returned to him. Of course, there's always lengthy litigation open to you."

"You mean, make a court fight of it?" Charlie asked.

"Yes," Sessler said.

"I hardly think it'll come to that," Charlie Two-Moon said. "I'm doing this for Carney because he doesn't want the boys to be alone."

"That's what I understood," Sessler said, then moved to the swinging gate and stepped out into the waiting area. He shook hands. "It's good to see you again, Charlie."

He went on down the hall and Charlie and the sheriff went back to the jail and both men were released. Holbrook smiled when he saw Charlie Two-Moon and he took back his property from the jailer, signed the receipt, then said, "God, it's awful in jail."

"I've got Doc's car outside," Charlie said. "Let's go."

Fred Teeter was stuffing his wallet into his back pocket. "Hey, what about me?"

"What about you?" Charlie asked.

"Well, how do I get back?"

"How did you get here?" Charlie asked and walked out.

They went to the parked car and got in and Fred Teeter hurried out. He put his foot on the running board and said, "God dammit, it won't hurt you to give me a ride."

"Get your foot off the car," Charlie said.

Teeter glared. "Damned Indian," he said and stepped back as Charlie backed out of the parking lot and drove on out of town.

Jim Holbrook leaned his head against the door glass and said, "I couldn't sleep last night. A drunk was snoring next door and another sang all night. Teeter walked up and down his cell all night." Then he looked at Charlie Two-Moon. "You're the best friend I've ever had, Charlie. I mean that."

"Forget it."

"No, I can't forget it," Holbrook said. "I'm not going to forget it either. I'd have killed him if you hadn't stopped me."

Charlie shook his head. "No, you wouldn't

have killed him, Jim. You were hurt and mad, but you wouldn't have killed him. You wanted him to crawl, that was all."

"I had a gun," Holbrook said. "And I intended to use it."

"Why didn't you when he let go with the shotgun?" He turned his head and looked at Holbrook. "Jim, I've killed men. I know how hard it is, how sick it makes you, and how much it bothers a man. It's something you never forget."

"I just can't get it set in my mind that she's gone," Holbrook said. He patted his pockets for tobacco and found that he had none so Charlie offered him his sack of Durham and Holbrook rolled a cigarette. "You've never wanted a woman so you wouldn't—"

"Why wouldn't I?" Charlie said quickly. They looked at each other. "Jim, people never expect an Indian or a nigger to feel anything or to want anything. Think, man. We're all alone in our own way."

"I guess that's right," Holbrook said. "It's not good, is it?" Then he smiled. "I saw that teacher from the reservation going your way one day. She was drivin' like she had something definite in mind. Something in the wind there, Charlie?"

"Enough to get up a man's hopes," Charlie Two-Moon said. "Mine, anyway."

When he reached town, he parked Carney's car and went up the stairs to the office. The doctor was reading the paper and Charlie said, "Some emergency."

"Well, there was," Carney said. "Didn't last long though." He shook hands with Holbrook. "Now that you've had a taste of jail, stay out of them."

"My exact intention," Holbrook said. "Doc, Teeter's boys—"

"They're going to stay with Charlie for a while," Carney said. "Sessler called me about an hour ago from the county seat. Charlie, if you don't want to do this now I—"

"I told you I would," Charlie Two-Moon said. "Getting cold feet, Doc?"

"Well, it's just dawned on me that I've taken on considerable responsibility, making the recommendation and all." He glanced briefly at Charlie. "I—ah—called Martha Frank. She said she'd come over as soon as her school let out." Charlie opened his mouth and Carney cut him off. "Well, I thought a woman's touch at a time like this— Oh, hell, never mind what I thought."

Charlie Two-Moon spoke without anger. "Doc, is there anybody's business you wouldn't stick your nose into?"

"Guess not," Carney said. "Hell, why don't you marry that girl? She's just waiting to be asked."

"You're an authority on marriage?"

"Yes, I am," Carney said stoutly. "It's true I've been a single man all my life, but as a doctor,

124

I've observed marriage carefully, and I might add, with a certain clinical detachment. I heartily recommend it."

"You used to recommend sulfur and molasses," Charlie said. Then his irritation left him and he laughed. "Tell me something: why the devil don't I cross a nosey old fud like you right out of my life?"

"Because you like me," Carney said. "Beneath that know-it-all, I'm-my-own-man and to-hell-with-what-the-world-thinks attitude, there beats a heart as big as a watermelon." Carney filled and lighted his pipe. "You ought to thank me, Charlie. I'm making you participate in life, not merely spectate." Then he thought of something. "Where the hell is Fred Teeter?"

"The last I saw," Holbrook said, "he was standing on the sidewalk cussing Indians." Then his manner turned serious. "I guess we should have given him a ride, Charlie. The man's got enough hate in him without some more building up." He started to button his coat. "I guess I'd better get back to my place. The stock ain't been fed and I've let everything go to hell. A man ought to have a better grip on himself than that." He reached up and touched Charlie Two-Moon on the shoulder. "Thanks, Charlie. You too, Doc."

"Jim, you get into town once in a while now," Carney said. "Don't you go brooding out there."

"All right," Holbrook said and went out.

"I wasted my breath there," Carney said. "Too bad." He reached for his coat and hat and a muffler to put around his neck. "Isn't there a woman somewhere around here he can get interested in?"

Charlie Two-Moon laughed. "Is that your only prescription for taking a man's mind off his troubles?"

"Know a better one?" Carney asked. "Let's go get the boys."

11

Doctor Oswald Carney had few patients from two o'clock on, so he sat by his office window and watched the movement on the street. The sun was bright and rapidly drying the slush left over from the winter; only a few patches of wetness remained on the street, and these were in the low spots along the curb.

He watched the cars drive up and down, then his attention centered on a new Chevrolet sedan that pulled into a parking place in front of the bank. Since he recognized the car, he expected Jules Kerrick to get out and was surprised to see Martha Frank.

She looked up at his window then came up the stairs, entered his outer office and knocked on his door.

"It's always open," Carney said. "We have nothing to hide." She came in and took off her gloves and unbuttoned her short jacket. Carney smiled, "So the government finally broke down and bought the agency a car. Don't tell me you're feeling ill?"

"Never felt better," Martha said. "But I did want to talk to you, Doctor."

"Now that's something I do well," Carney said. "I've always been a brilliant conversationalist. You don't mind if I smoke?"

"Not at all," Martha said. "Have you seen Charlie lately?"

"It's been a month," Carney said. "Something wrong?"

"Doctor, you know this is all wrong." She smoothed her gloves and hesitated as though wondering just how she would say what she had to say. "Those boys belong with their father."

"He's turning into the town drunk," Carney said bluntly. "His farm's going to hell and I can't say that I'm sorry."

"I wish you were," Martha said. "Doctor, you can't do this to that man. You have no right to do it. It doesn't matter what he is, or what he's done. The boys are his and they belong with him."

"Now that's an opinion," Carney said. "Mine against yours."

"Yes it is, and I'm just as right as you are."

Carney shrugged. "This is going to take us in circles."

"All right. Why Charlie? Of all the people in town, surely—"

"Because he's strong," Carney said. "Because he knows trouble. Because Fred Teeter is afraid of him. Maybe that's why he drinks, because he's afraid to act, and drinking makes him forget he's afraid."

"You can't use a man like that to get what you want," Martha said. She leaned back in her chair and studied Carney carefully. "I just can't make up my mind what you're really after. If it's Fred Teeter—"

Carney waved his hand absently. "I should be insulted that you even think that. No, Teeter doesn't really matter to me one way or another." He fell silent for a moment. "Why do people have to waste themselves, Martha?"

"I don't understand."

"Well, look at Holbrook; he loved Teeter's wife—all that was wasted. And Charlie, he—"

"All that is none of your business," Martha snapped.

"I've made it my business."

"I don't think you can do that," Martha said. "Doctor, I thought you were Charlie's friend."

"Why, I am."

"Then get those two boys out of his house. Get them out before there's real trouble over it. Stop trying to hand down punishments to people. They're not yours to punish."

Carney arched an eyebrow. "Is that what I'm doing?"

"Yes," Martha said, standing. "Doctor, I think you've saved too many lives; you're beginning to think you're God. Come out to the reservation and assist Doctor Parker. He loses far more than he saves." Then she smiled. "I know, you regard him as a drunk. He does drink, to excess, but I can't blame him. I don't think a man, any man, who remained totally sober, could face the continued failures that he does."

She was a little angry when she left and got in the car and she was sorry for this for she hadn't meant to be, yet it was the knowledge that she hadn't made any impression at all on Carney that discouraged her.

She had some things to order from town, and she stopped at several stores and by the time she drove out, the back seat was piled with boxes.

Charlie Two-Moon was working outside when she drove into his yard and he put down his hammer and bag of nails and went over to the car. Now that the weather had turned mild, he was building his outside hutches and sawdust clung to the hair on the back of his hands and sweat soaked his shirt.

"I got everything but the wire," Martha said. "That'll come from a hardware supply house in Omaha." She heard a tractor laboring and looked past the barn to the west sixty. Jim Holbrook was astride his Fordson, busy breaking ground with a two-bottom plow.

He unloaded the car and carried the boxes inside and she put the canned goods on the pantry shelves while he washed at the pump. When he came in, she had coffee hot and the cups set out.

"The boys ought to be coming home from school pretty soon," he said.

His manner of speaking, dry and noncommittal, drew her attention.

"Nothing's changed?"

He shook his head. "They take to Joe all right. Somehow a little Indian is different from a big Indian." He sat down and slapped his hand against the tabletop. "This is where it all starts, listening to Papa talk about those damned niggers and those dirty Indians and those cheap Jews. Right here, at the kitchen table. You put an idea into a young mind and it's kind of set for good. Later, a man's judgment may change it, but it's still there, asleep, waiting to pop up again." He smiled and shook his head. "Until I went into the army, I thought everyone just hated Indians. It was quite a surprise to find that there were priest-loving Micks in the world, and dirty Polacks, and Pennsylvania Hunkies, and Chicago Kikes. That's where I learned to live with all this, Martha. It occurred to me that it wasn't really hate at all. Just intolerance. That's why Teeter's boys don't get under my skin. That's why Teeter and his friends never really bother me."

She poured the coffee and sat down. "I talked to Carney in town, Charlie." She looked at him and found him watching her. "Well maybe I shouldn't have, but I just had to say my piece."

"It didn't do any good," he said. "It never has."

131

He leaned back and put an arm over the back of the chair. "I lived with him for four years, Martha. He gets his way, somehow."

"Why?"

Charlie Two-Moon shrugged. "I used to wonder. I don't anymore. I went to school dances because Carney wanted me to. He pushed me on people, wrangled me invitations, and somehow he makes them like it."

"Not like it," Martha said. "They do it, but they don't really like it. And it's bad, Charlie. Do you see that?"

He nodded. "The night I first came back from the army, he insisted I go to a dance the people were giving for the boys. I knew how it would be."

"And so did he," she said quickly. "Charlie, Teeter's boys belong with him."

"Yes, I thought so all along."

"Then why didn't you stand up to him, Charlie?"

"I don't know," he admitted. "I suppose I'll have to find an answer for that."

"Sooner or later," she said. Then she laughed and reached into her purse. "I got a letter from my father and mother. They'd like to know if early March would be a good time to visit." She reached across the table and took his hands in hers. "Charlie, you'll like them. And they'll like you."

"It seems advisable," Charlie said, "to get off to a good start with ones future in-laws." Then he laughed. "March is fine."

A car came down the road, then there was a rending of metal and both of them hurried to the back door. From their porch they could see what had happened; the car had failed to make the turn into Charlie's yard and had crunched against his stout gate posts.

Martha Frank said, "Isn't that Fred Teeter's car?"

"Let's go have a look," he said and stepped off the porch.

As they came up, Teeter was getting out and his foot slipped off the running board and he fell, but got up.

Charlie Two-Moon said, "You're drunk, Fred."

He looked carefully, trying to focus his eyes. "I'm a little," he said, slurring the words. "Come to see my sons." He was holding onto the door of the car and he swayed in a wide circle, like some boy playfully revolving around a flagpole. Then he bumped into the fender and stopped.

"You come on in the house," Charlie said. "I'll get you some coffee."

"Come to see my sons," Teeter said again.

"Sure, sure," Charlie said soothingly, and helped him into the car. "But we'll get you straightened up a little first. All right?" He slid behind the wheel and backed the car, then

133

cramped the wheels so it would clear the gate post. Martha stood on the running board as he drove on to the house and they both helped Fred Teeter from the car.

The man needed a shave and a bath, and when Martha looked at Charlie she wrinkled her nose and rolled her eyes. Charlie took him on the screened porch and made him sit down while Martha went inside to heat some water. When Charlie put the large wooden tub on the floor, Fred Teeter roused a bit and said, "Whazzat?"

"I'm going to give you a bath," Charlie said. "You haven't been taking very good care of yourself, Fred."

"Whole worl's gone to hell," Teeter said. "Boom!" He flung his arms wide and Charlie ducked and laughed and began to undress him. He called inside to Martha. "Get some clean clothes out of my dresser drawer. I'll call you when I'm through. You can set out my razor too."

She brought the things and laid them on the wash bench, then went into the parlor and waited while Charlie made Teeter scrub himself. The bath sobered him a little, but not enough so he could be trusted with a straight razor; Charlie shaved him, made him dry off and dress and go into the kitchen.

Martha came back and poured some coffee and while Charlie forced it down Teeter, she went out to the porch, emptied the water, and threw away the man's clothes. By the time she came back, Teeter could sit straight and the slur was leaving his voice.

She reached for the coffeepot and Charlie said, "He's on his third one. How do you feel, Fred?"

"Better," he said. He glanced at both of them, then studied the pattern in the oilcloth. "My boys didn't see me this way, did they?"

"No," Charlie said. He turned and looked at the alarm clock sitting atop the kitchen stove. "They'll be here in another twenty minutes."

"I'll be all right by then," Teeter said. "You're a white man, Charlie, helpin' me like this. You could pick up that phone and put me in hot water."

"What reason would I have for doing that?" Charlie asked.

Fred Teeter shook his head. "I ain't allowed to see 'em, you know. Carney fixed that for me. But twice now I've come out toward evenin' and saw 'em playing in the yard. I guess they're happy here."

"They'd be happier with you," Martha said. "You're their father."

Teeter put his head in his hands and shook it slowly. "What am I going to do, Charlie? Did I kill her? Some say that. How long does a man have to pay?" He raised his head as Jim Holbrook

135

drove his tractor into the barnyard and stopped it. "I don't want to see him, Charlie!"

"You can't keep putting it off," Charlie said. He went to the door as Holbrook stepped onto the porch, then he came in, a bottle of brandy in his hand.

He looked at Fred Teeter but Teeter was starting across the room. "I never knew you to drink good stuff," Holbrook said. He put the bottle on the edge of the sink and Charlie Two-Moon looked at it, then at Holbrook. "The back door of his car was open and it'd rolled out on the ground. That's not the local bootleg stuff, I can tell you that. Came in by boat from Cuba after traveling halfway around the world; five dollars a bottle is my guess." He went to the waterbucket and sank the dipper, then turned and leaned against the sink. "What's the matter, Fred, can't you look at me?"

"No," Teeter said.

Holbrook said, "I've been wondering how I'd feel when I saw you face to face. I don't feel anything, except being a little sorry for you."

"The best thing you could have done for me," Teeter said, "would been to have pulled that trigger when you had the chance." He had to work at it, but he forced himself to look at Jim Holbrook. "What are they trying to make of me, Jim? Am I so worthless that nobody cares? Was I so bad that people could just—just throw me away like they didn't want me anymore?" He shook his head. "If I don't find that out, I'm going to go crazy."

"You've got to start by laying off the booze," Charlie said. "Where did you get this, Fred? Mel Allen sell it to you?"

"No, no. Allen never handles good stuff," Teeter said. "It was in my car. Two bottles. Someone's been puttin' the stuff in my car." He moved his shoulders. "Under the seat, in the door pocket; every time I park it somewhere."

"Somebody's got a kind heart," Holbrook said softly. "Or else they like to see a man good and drunk." Through the open screen door came the sound of young laughter, and Joe Teel rode the horse to the barn, the two Teeter boys mounted behind him.

On Fred Teeter's face there was a slack, stricken look. He said, "Charlie, my God, what do I say?"

"You'll know what to say," Charlie said. "Go on out there."

Teeter left his chair and went to the door, then he stepped outside and off the porch. Charlie turned to the stove and poured a cup of coffee, then he heard the boys yell, "Daddy, Daddy!" and he looked at Jim Holbrook and Martha Frank.

"That's a good sound," he said. "Maybe the best sound there is."

"When a man gets to thinking another man's all

bad, maybe he ought to listen for somethin' like that," Holbrook said. Then he took a deep breath and turned to the door. "Still some plowing to do before dark."

He opened the door and stopped when Charlie spoke. "It's not a thing to be sad about, Jim. She was always his, right up to the minute she died."

"I know that now," he said. "It's all right now."

12

Charlie Two-Moon invited Fred Teeter to stay for supper, and Martha Frank cooked a pot roast while Charlie went to tend his rabbits. Teeter went along and carried feed and pitched hay and it was almost dark by the time they were finished. As they started from the barn a car turned into Charlie's yard, and Fred Teeter stayed in the barn while Charlie went to see who it was.

Ray Andrews got down, but left the lights on. He had parked beside Teeter's damaged car and when Charlie came up, Andrews said, "I got a report that Fred Teeter's drunk again. A man shouldn't drive in that condition." He lifted his foot and kicked the wrinkled fender. "The man's getting out of hand, Charlie."

"I drove the car in from the road," Charlie Two-Moon said. "I figured someone might come along tonight and plow into it." He put his hands in his pockets and waited; Andrews kicked the tires and opened and closed the door.

"Do you understand what a court order is, Charlie?"

"Yes."

"Teeter's under a court order to stay away from

his boys. If he's caught disobeying that he can go to jail or be fined." Andrews shook his head. "And Teeter's about broke. He's let his farm go to hell and he's spent a lot on booze."

"You ought to go after some of those bootleggers," Charlie said.

"Now I run my office pretty well," Andrews said. "Are you going to tell me where he is?"

"Not if I can help it," Charlie said. "Sheriff, if you arrest him, I'll go his bail. Jim Holbrook will chip in with me."

Andrews frowned. "I don't understand that. You hate Teeter. So does Jim." He blew a gust of breath through his nose. "Hell, Jim tried to kill Teeter!"

"If he'd really tried, he'd have done it," Charlie said. He looked carefully at Andrews. "Did you see Teeter drunk?"

"No, as a matter of fact, someone called me."

"Who?"

"Well now, if I revealed my source of information, people would stop trusting me to keep a confidence." He shook his head. "Why are you protecting him, Charlie? I don't understand that."

"Because he needs it now."

"Some months ago you knocked him out in Scarbrough's store. Now you say he needs protection."

"Some months ago he needed knocking down," Charlie said. "Things change. People change."

"So it seems," Andrews said. "All right, Charlie, I'm going to let this go this time. But the next time I come out here, I'll have a search warrant with me. No hard feelings, but I've got to do my job." He turned and got in his car, but held the door open. "You tell Teeter to straighten up. He's never going to find a decent woman to marry unless he does, and that's how he'll get those kids back, to make a home for them."

"That's bad justice," Charlie said.

Ray Andrews shrugged. "Charlie, for sixteen years I've been enforcing the laws and some have been bad, but I can't change it. Maybe Doc Carney acted in haste. I thought so at the time, but he has influence." He ground the starter, backed the car around, and drove out to the road and turned toward town.

Fred Teeter came from the barn and met Charlie Two-Moon by the well curbing. "I heard what he said. Charlie, it ain't right. Why do people work hard at hurting other people?"

"You tell me why. You did."

"God, I just don't know," Teeter said. "But people are always putting thoughts into your head, and sometimes after you've said something you realize those weren't your own words at all, but something someone pounded into you."

"Then you ought to pick your friends more carefully," Charlie said. "Better say good night to your boys, Fred."

"All right," Teeter said and started to walk away. Then he stopped. "You've treated me white, Charlie. And I guess it wasn't easy."

"No, it really wasn't," Charlie said frankly, "but I've found that most good things aren't easy."

Teeter kept the windows down on the way and the cool spring air cleared the last residue of his drunk out of his head. It had been a good evening and he felt full of resolve; by golly, he could lick this drinking. Other men had.

When he turned into his gate he saw that it was broken and lying on the ground and remembered that he'd driven through it one night without bothering to get out and swing it, and he told himself that he'd have to repair that in the morning. His place was run down; he'd let everything go, even sold off his livestock, and in his fields there was not one plowed furrow.

His headlights picked up a car parked by his porch and he stopped and got out and walked toward it. Then he recognized it and said, "What you doing here, Doc?"

"I heard you were drunk," Carney said. "I thought maybe you'd hurt yourself. And besides, you didn't come to see me last week. Your clap dried up all right?"

"Yeah," Teeter said and crossed his porch. He kicked some litter out of the way and went inside and the odor hit him; he'd have to scrub the place from top to bottom.

He lighted a lamp and Carney came in, closing the door with his foot. He looked around and said, "You live like a pig, Fred."

"It's pretty dirty all right," Teeter said. "In the morning I'll scrub it out. Things are going to be different."

The lamplight reflected in Carney's glasses. "How different?"

"I've swore off the bottle."

"Really?" Carney said. "I didn't know you had that much strength of character." He took off his hat, whipped dust from the cushion of a chair and sat down. "You'll be drunk by tomorrow noon. Do you know what it's like to quit? You'll get the shakes and your stomach will turn inside out, craving for a drink. You'll climb these walls, Teeter. Now, you're a boozer. I knew it the way you went after the stuff. Somehow it's a fitting role for you, a drunk, living like a pig. Men who use women, Teeter, are pigs. They should sleep in their mess and eat from a trough."

Fred Teeter stared at Carney, shocked at the coldness in the man's voice. "Doc, why do you hate me?"

"I don't know as you'll understand this, Teeter, but woman is the fairest flower in God's garden. Without them we'd all be animals. You don't trample flowers, Teeter." Then he laughed. "I knew you wouldn't understand. You went to Charlie Two-Moon's to see the boys, didn't you?"

"What if I did?" Teeter flared. "Charlie didn't treat me like trash."

"Charlie is an Indian," Carney said. "An Indian who forgives easily because he learned early that if he didn't, he'd be hating everyone on earth by the time he was twenty-one. And of course you kissed his feet, curried his favor." Carney's voice was full of scorn. "Teeter, you're so gutless that you make me sick. You don't even have the backbone to hate a man with consistency."

Teeter came over and stood before Carney with his arms outspread. "What do you want to keep on punishing me for, Doc? You're a cruel bastard. Ain't you ever going to let up?"

Carney leaned back in his chair and looked at Teeter. "You ought to go out to the reservation and buy a squaw. You'll have to do it quietly because Kerrick doesn't allow that kind of business."

"What are you saying?" Teeter asked, aghast.

"I'm telling you how to get a woman," Carney said, "and believe me, it's about the best you'll get around here." Then he smiled. "Have a good time with the boys? Missed them, I know, especially in the few sober moments you've had. I'm a man who'd go by the letter of the law, Teeter. Marry again and you'll get your boys back."

Teeter walked up and down the room and at every swing to reverse direction he looked at Oswald Carney. Then he stopped and said, "You took Charlie Two-Moon off the reservation, gave him a place to live while he went to school. Now I wonder why, Doc."

"Generosity," Carney said. "I liked the boy."

"You hated his guts," Teeter said flatly. "You hate Indians."

"I see all the whiskey hasn't worn off," Carney said dryly.

"I'm sober as a judge," Teeter snapped. "Yeah, real sober. Doc, I don't understand it. Me, somehow me, I got something triggered off and I don't know what it is. But I'm going to cross you, Doc. I'm going to keep you from getting what you want. And you know how I'm going to do it? I'm going to stay sober. I don't have the money to buy rotgut and I've taken the pledge."

"Courageously spoken," Carney said and stood up. "I hope you live up to it, Teeter."

"Like hell you do," Teeter said and went to the door. He stood by it and Carney shrugged and went out and before he got off the porch, Teeter slammed the door and shot the bolt.

He was angry and it drove him to activity and suddenly he could not stand the litter and filth a moment longer so he built the kitchen fire and put on buckets of water to heat. He opened both doors and, with a broom, went after the dust and papers and scatter of trash, pushing it all outside into a pile. Then he set fire to it and went to work scrubbing the house.

When he got hungry he cooked some eggs and ate them, then went back to the job, working until the small hours of the morning. He was tired but it was a good feeling and it kept him from thinking about a drink; Teeter told himself that it didn't matter because he had nothing to drink for he vaguely remembered Jim Holbrook taking the bottle out of the car and leaving it on Charlie Two-Moon's sink.

But before dawn the thirst was there, just as Carney had said it would be, a burning in his stomach and a dryness of the throat. His hands shook a little and his head ached and he drank water but it really didn't do any good.

When it was daylight he went outside and pumped the watering trough full of water and took off his clothes and bathed in it, and the cold water sent chills through him and for a time it helped, but he dried off and dressed and the ache, the longing came back.

He fought it for a while, then gave in to it and went to his car and had a look, just in case he'd been mistaken. He took up the back seat and felt around, then he found it, a full bottle wedged between the cushions of the front seat.

Teeter felt like crying and he stood there, hugging the bottle, torn between his maddening thirst and the promise he had made. He took the bottle inside and put it on the kitchen table and tried not to look at it but it was a magnet drawing his eyes.

He argued with himself, pleaded, made new promises, scrapped them, went back to his original intention, changed his mind; for two hours he whip-sawed himself raw. Once he broke the seal, intending to have a drink, but he put the bottle down.

He took the cork out and fought that off, replacing it, but he knew he was losing, knew Carney was right, that he didn't have the stuff to stick it out.

It was a terrible thing to know about yourself, that you were vile, without virtue, and this knowledge broke Teeter; he uncorked the bottle, upended it, and there was no turning back.

He sat at the table and drank himself into a stupor and messed himself and slept in his mess and when he woke it was night and the lamp was on and a part of his mind wondered how that could be because he had turned it out at daybreak.

Then he opened his eyes and saw Carney standing by the door.

"I told you," Carney said softly. "Don't you believe anyone, Fred?" Then he laughed and put a match to his cigar. "I see you cleaned the place. Very nice. But you've soiled yourself. A pity. Nothing ever comes out well for you, does it?"

Teeter rolled over on his back and looked at the ceiling. "You put the bottle in my car," he said wearily. "Kill me, Doc!"

"What a terrible thing to say. I've never taken a life." He took another bottle from his overcoat pocket and placed it on the table. "You can get through the day on this one. I've got to go out to the reservation and help Parker with an operation; the man will surely bungle it if I don't. On my way back I'll stop in and see you. If you've killed the bottle, I have another with me."

"I'd like to kill you," Teeter said and tried to sit up but he couldn't do it.

Carney laughed softly. "You're full of terrible thoughts, Fred. While I'm at the reservation shall I look around and see if I can find some woman for you? You're a rough man so she'd have to be strong. Not one of those graceful fawns. Someone a little hefty, with hips—"

"Nononono," Fred Teeter said, shaking his head. "Doc, I can't think good now." He opened his mouth and breathed heavily. "But all night, when I worked, I thought about you. You can't be punishing me for what I did, but for what someone else did to you."

"Leave it to a drunk to come up with nonsense," Carney said. "This is retribution, Teeter. Sort of like the hand of God." He buttoned his coat. "Well, I don't want to be late. Parker worries and when he worries, he drinks. Not like you do; the man doesn't seek oblivion, just to remove the sharpest, most injurious edges of worldly truth."

Carney went out to his car, puffing on his cigar, then he rolled his tongue around in his mouth, dissatisfied with the sour taste and shied it into the yard. It struck the well curbing in a shower of sparks and he got into his car and drove away.

He drove rather fast and his knuckles were white as he gripped the wheel, and finally he lifted his foot off the accelerator, braked gently and parked, breathing deeply until he calmed himself. It made him ill to look at Fred Teeter, yet he knew he would go back, and back again until the man destroyed himself; there was simply no other way, no other justice but destruction.

A new cigar tasted good to him and he put a match to it, then rolled the window down to throw it out. He looked back then and saw the smoke and he couldn't quite believe it was coming from the Teeter place. But it was and for a moment he simply stared at it, then the thought hit him that his cast aside cigar had caught in some of the rubbish Teeter had swept into the yard, some that hadn't been gathered and burned.

Then he got out of the car, thinking that that was a big pall of smoke for mere rubbish. A strong breeze blew against him, lifting the edge of his coat and he realized that the rubbish must have blown against the dry planks of the porch.

"The house is going," Carney said aloud and

hopped into the car, meaning to turn around and go back. Then he stopped a moment, put the car in gear and drove on to the reservation.

He didn't look back again.

13

Jules Kerrick met Doctor Carney at the reservation's dispensary. Martha Frank was there, and the patient's family, a brood of dark-faced stoics who were plainly wishing they'd let the medicine man handle this. Parker came out in his shirt sleeves, ready to scrub up and he was quite sober. He shook hands with Carney and said, "Glad you could assist, Doctor. Bad fracture here. Compound of course. The left tibia is badly shattered, and the fibula is a splinter fracture." He looked at the Indians sitting there. "Damned savages. The boy fell in the rocks yesterday, early in the afternoon as I understand it. This morning, when he failed to appear at school, Miss Frank investigated. I called you soon after." He shook his head. "If we don't have gangrene here—" He took Carney's arm. "Please step this way. The patient's prepared. Miss Frank will administer the anesthetic."

They went into his office and through it to the small operating room and Carney took off his coat, rolled his sleeves, and began to scrub up. The patient was on the table, and a lay nurse bathed his forehead.

Carney looked around at Martha Frank. "I have another bag of instruments in my car. Would you get them for me, please?"

"Certainly," Martha said and went out.

Carney's coupé was parked around the corner of the building and she opened the door on the passenger side and looked in the luggage space behind the seat. His bag was jammed in a corner and held there by a wadded blanket and she pushed this aside. Then she saw the bottle and for a moment she could not think where she had seen it before, then it came to her that this was a twin to the one Jim Holbrook had placed on Charlie Two-Moon's kitchen sink.

She hesitated, struck by the impulse to take it along, then she rolled it aside, covered it with the blanket and went inside with the instrument case. Carney was scrubbed and masked, and she emptied the instruments into the sterilizer and scrubbed before getting into a gown and mask.

When she moved around to the head of the table and started to give the boy the ether, Carney was busy and paying no attention to her.

There was no time for talk, or for questions.

She was not a trained nurse, yet she had some schooling and a good deal of experience and she could not help but compare Carney with Parker, who was a good doctor, yet by comparison, seemed almost clumsy.

Carney was fast and accurate and his fingers were sure and he wasted no motion at all. Parker had invited Carney to assist, but it was Parker who was assisting, handing Carney instruments, standing back while this talented man worked.

The operation took longer than Martha Frank expected, yet she knew it was shorter by an hour over what Parker could have done. The boy's leg was finally placed in a cast, and in traction, and he was wheeled, bed and all, into the hall and into the six-bed hospital at the end of the building.

Carney let Parker do this while he stood there, stripping off his gown and staring at the patient's relatives.

"Which of you are the parents of this boy?" Carney asked.

They looked at him for a moment, then a man stood up, and a woman. Carney threw his gown on the floor. "You fools! Won't you ever learn? Is there no way to reach you at all?"

Martha Frank stepped out of the doctor's office; she stopped in the doorway and saw Carney's anger and the impassive faces of the boy's parents. "You won't get anywhere that way," she said calmly.

"I wasn't asking you," Carney said brusquely.

"I was volunteering the information," she said.

He looked at her then. "Can't a man express displeasure around here?"

"There is no point in telling them that you think they're stupid," Martha said. "They already know what you think."

He stood there as though he meant to make a real argument of this, then he made a cutting motion with his hand and stepped outside. When she heard him walk to the far end of the porch, she said, "Go home, Chee Tani. The boy will be all right."

There was no change in the man's expression. "Will he walk well? Will he be able to tend his sheep?"

"Yes," she said. "He'll be well and strong again."

"That's good," Chee Tani said. "We are poor and we must all work hard." He took his wife and relatives and left the building. She followed them outside and saw Jules Kerrick talking to Parker and Carney and walked over to them. Kerrick's manner was excited and he broke off in the middle of his talk. "Martha, I was telling them about the fire. Fred Teeter's place went up in smoke. I got the call from town while you were operating on the boy."

"I suppose I'll be needed there," Carney said.

Kerrick shook his head. "They haven't found Teeter. Talk is that he got caught inside."

"How horrible," Martha said. "Mr. Kerrick, may I use your car?"

"Of course," he said. "I can't leave here now."

He reached in his pocket for the keys and handed them to her. She turned and went into the building to change her clothes and get a coat, and when she came out and got into Kerrick's car, he was still talking to Carney and Parker.

She drove faster than usual and as she neared the Teeter place she could still see a thin wisp of smoke rising and cars were parked haphazardly and the two county fire trucks were there, but the firemen were rolling up their hoses; there was nothing left of the house but a crumbled portion of the fireplace, a half-melted iron bedstead, and the kitchen stove marked the location of the kitchen.

The firemen had managed to save the barn and two of the outbuildings, and she saw Charlie Two-Moon and Jim Holbrook helping the firemen stack their hose. When she stopped the car and got out, one of the fire trucks drove away, followed by Sheriff Ray Andrews' car. The crowd was breaking up, going home; there was nothing to stay for, nothing to see except smoldering ashes and no one wanted to come across a charred body.

The last fire truck left and Charlie and Jim stood by the well curbing and she joined them there. She said, "This is a terrible thing. Did they find him?"

"No," Charlie Two-Moon said.

"How did it start?"

He shrugged. "Andrews thinks that maybe Teeter was drunk and upset a lamp."

She looked at him. "But you don't think that."

"Jim doesn't think that and he's convinced me," Charlie said.

Holbrook pointed to the burned grass and rubbish. "I saw the smoke right away and came over. The front of the house was going up fast and it had already spread over the roof to the back. About then the firemen got here, but there was no saving it. But I was the first one here and the grass and rubbish had burnt itself out." He pointed to the ground where he stood. "Here's where I think the fire started, outside the house near the well curbing."

"Which means," Charlie said, "that if Teeter started it, he had to be outside." He took out his tobacco and rolled a smoke. His hands and face were grimy and there were singes on his cuffs and spark holes in his shirt. Holbrook was even dirtier. "The firemen probed the ashes some, but they didn't find anything. Which could mean that Teeter ran off."

"Or still be in there," Holbrook said. "I couldn't sleep not knowing, Charlie."

"The fire's pretty hot to be poking around."

Holbrook nodded. "The firemen left a lot of gunny sacks. If we soaked 'em in the horse trough and wrapped 'em around our feet and legs—"

"That ought to do it," Charlie said and started to gather the sacks. They wrapped themselves well, then submerged in the watering trough and stepped out dripping wet. Using long sticks, they methodically probed and stirred the ashes and now and then came out to redunk themselves in the watering trough. For several hours they sifted through the ruin of Teeter's house and found nothing, and Martha waited and watched and hoped their search would be fruitless.

When they came back to wet themselves for the eighth time, Charlie Two-Moon said, "Jim, let's talk this over. We've been through the place pretty carefully, but I keep getting the feeling that we've missed something."

"I wouldn't know what it would be," Holbrook said.

"Well, suppose you were in your house, asleep, and you woke to find the place burning all around you. What would you do?"

"That's supposin' Teeter was inside."

"Let's figure that he was."

Holbrook scratched his head. "I'd head for the root cel—" He stopped and stared at Charlie Two-Moon. "Hell, yes, the root cellar. There ain't a farm around here that don't have a root cellar." He splashed into the trough ahead of Charlie and they went to the kitchen area and probed with their poles until they found a spot where the floor gave way to a hole, then they kicked ashes and debris aside and found the root cellar door, partially burned through.

Holbrook got it open and jumped down. The place was full of foul air, hot, with a bed of ashes that had sifted through heaped around his feet. Charlie followed him and they let their eyes adjust to the darkness. The root cellar was an eight-by-twelve room, lined with fieldstone, and they searched the corners and there they found Fred Teeter, unconscious, but apparently unhurt.

He had managed to cover himself with bags full of potatoes and rutabagas before passing out.

They shouldered him up and Charlie got out first to pull him up and together they carried him clear of the house and put him down by the watering trough.

"He don't look burned," Jim Holbrook said. "I guess the heat and foul air got him."

They bathed Teeter's face and finally he came around and opened his eyes. He looked at Charlie Two-Moon, then reached up and touched his face, the way a child will, to assure himself that all is really well.

Then Fred Teeter sat there and silently cried without shame or embarrassment.

"We'll put him in my car," Holbrook said. "Your place is closest, Charlie."

"Fine, I'll give you a hand. Just put your arm around me there, Fred." He lifted Teeter and helped him into Holbrook's car, then turned to

Martha Frank. "My horse will go on home by himself. Can I ride on the running board?" He looked at his sodden, ruined clothes. "I wouldn't want to ruin Kerrick's new car."

He rode the running board and she followed Jim Holbrook and fifteen minutes later they pulled into Charlie's yard. The boys ran out and climbed on the cars and Holbrook shooed them off, and Teeter walked into the house under his own power, his sons tagging along, asking questions about the fire.

Joe Teel stood with Charlie Two-Moon. "They wanted to go see the fire but I wouldn't allow it. There were chores to be done, and I told them you would tell them what happened."

"You're a good man, Joe. Watch for the horse; he'll be wandering in soon." He reached out and mussed the boy's hair. "Now run in the house and bring me some clean clothes. I'm going to take a bath under the pump—" He glanced at Martha Frank. "—Whether you watch or not."

"I'm going in," she said, and hurried off.

Later, around coffee and some sandwiches, Fred Teeter said, "I broke my word to you, Charlie. I got drunk again."

Holbrook rolled his eyes. "Did you have a bottle stashed?"

Teeter shook his head. "I have a friend who keeps me supplied." He looked at Holbrook, then at Charlie Two-Moon, and lifted his coffee cup.

"Well?" Holbrook asked.

"He doesn't want to say," Martha said. "Can't you see that?"

"I can see it," Holbrook said, a bit irritated. "But I don't see why."

"Because of Charlie," she said. "Teeter doesn't want to say that Doctor Carney's been giving him the bottles. He knows how Charlie feels about Carney." They all stared at her as though they didn't believe her. "Quite innocently I found a bottle in Carney's car while he was at the reservation."

"So he likes a snort," Charlie said. "What does that mean?"

Martha looked at Fred Teeter. "Are you going to say anything?"

"I just can't," Teeter said, shaking his head. "Charlie's treated me like a white man and I just can't pay him back that way."

"Now wait a minute," Charlie said. "You can't half finish a thing like that. If you've got something to say, then say it."

"Carney hates me," Teeter said.

"That's no news," Charlie said. "As long as I've known him he's had it in for no-goods and wife-beaters. Carney has some strong opinions of people, Fred, and generally, he doesn't think too much of the human race."

"It's got to go deeper than that," Teeter said. "He wants me dead."

"So? There was a time when you said you'd kill me. You made talk in town," Charlie said. "What about that?"

"I didn't mean it."

"You said it."

"I know, but I didn't really mean it," Teeter said, raising his voice. Then he calmed himself. "Carney means it. He'll get me too. He came to my place, was waiting for me when I left here last night. He told me I couldn't stay off the bottle and I swore I would. But by morning I had the snakes crawling on me and he showed up and gave me a bottle." He looked at Charlie Two-Moon and saw that he wasn't making much of an impression. "You don't believe me."

"Fred, you'd better face the facts," Charlie said. "Look at yourself and look at Carney. You've always been hell to get along with, even as a kid and age hasn't improved you much. All I ever got from you was a cuss and a kick. Compare that with a man who took me in, fed me, clothed me, sent me to school, helped me make something of myself instead of being just another lousy Indian. Now who do you think I'm going to believe?"

Fred Teeter nodded, not angry, just disappointed. "It figures, Charlie, and I don't blame you." He looked around at Martha Frank. "I told you I should have kept still."

"You did right," she said softly. Then she looked at Charlie Two-Moon. "But I've got to be

161

honest with you, Charlie. I believe Fred Teeter. Carney is no longer God to me."

"Why would he want to do this?" Charlie asked, waving his hands. "Just give me one good reason."

"I don't think any of us know the reasons," she said. "But I'm going to try to find out. You ought to too, Charlie, to settle it in your own mind."

"There's nothing to settle," he said and got up and poured another cup of coffee. Then he looked at Fred Teeter. "I want you to take your kids home." He held up his hand. "I don't give a damn about the court order. You'll always be trouble to me."

"I've got no house," Teeter said.

"Build one," Charlie told him. "Some of this tough luck might help straighten you up, get some of these crazy notions out of your head."

"Sure," Teeter said. "You've been a white man, Charlie, and I wouldn't argue about it." Then he sat there and studied his folded hands.

14

Jim Holbrook drove Teeter and the boys to his place; he had a tent that he was going to loan Teeter until he could build again, and after they left, Martha Frank cleaned the table and washed the dishes and she didn't say anything and Charlie Two-Moon knew she was holding it back.

Finally she said, "Charlie, that was a bad thing you did. By defying that court order you've as good as thrown him in jail."

"I guess that's so," he said and got up. He put on his coat and hat and she looked at him, puzzled.

"Where are you going?"

"To town. Do you think Jules would mind if I used his car? Of course if you want to go back—"

"I'll wait here," she said, studying his expression, his mood carefully. "Charlie, don't close me out."

"I wouldn't do that," he said and went out and got in the car. Teeter, he figured, had been having about as much bad luck as any one man could take, but now he wondered just how much luck it really was. As far as he was concerned, he didn't have much use for Teeter and never did have, but you had to draw the line somewhere; you couldn't go on disliking a man when he'd reached the end of the rope, and Fred Teeter had surely come to his.

He kept steering his thoughts away from Oswald Carney, but they kept coming back, pushing at him until he gave in. Martha hadn't been lying, and he guessed Teeter hadn't been either, but it wasn't easy to take someone's word in a matter like this. He wasn't sure he would be willing to accept it if Carney admitted it.

When he got to town he parked the car in the first convenient spot; everyone seemed to be talking about the fire, and Charlie hadn't seen this many people on the streets in midweek since the Armistice celebration.

A few stopped him to confirm the totality of Teeter's loss, and he told them it was all gone and went on to Carney's office. He went on up the stairs and found the door unlocked and went in.

Carney was in his office, standing by the window where he could look down at the street; he glanced around as Charlie came in, then motioned to a chair.

"Tragedy always draws a crowd," Carney said. "I was at the reservation when it happened." He turned away and went to his desk for a cigar and a match and he stood there, puffing thoughtfully.

164

"How do you feel about it?" Charlie asked quietly.

"How do I feel about what?"

"The fire."

"Bad," Carney said. "A hell of a way for a man to go." He walked back to the window and turned his attention on the street. "I heard the fire chief say that tomorrow he was going to go out there and sift the ashes when they'd cooled. I suppose I'll have to go along, unless the coroner comes down from the county seat."

"They won't find anything," Charlie said, "except maybe a busted whiskey bottle."

Carney turned his head and looked at Charlie Two-Moon. "I don't understand that. Not at all."

"It's simple," Charlie said. "Jim Holbrook and I dug Teeter out of the root cellar. He'd managed to crawl there, close the door and pile potatoes on top of him." He watched Carney's eyes and waited a moment before going on. "Did you set the place afire, Doc?"

"What a thing to say!"

"It didn't start from the inside," Charlie said softly. "Jim and I figured that out. You were there, Doc." He crossed his legs and put his hands behind his head. "You ought to be able to tell me why. That's all I'm asking."

"Tell you the why of what?"

"Why you want to kill Fred Teeter."

165

"Well, what earthly good is he?" Carney snapped. Then he looked at his cigar as though remembering he had it in his hand and puffed on it. "What have you got in mind, Charlie?"

"I don't know," Charlie Two-Moon said. "It depends on what you say."

"What do you want me to say?"

"That's up to you. If you want to think about it a minute, Teeter's got enough to go to the district attorney."

"That rumpot, what could he say that anyone would believe?"

"There's more," Charlie said. "Martha found a bottle in your car, the same kind of booze we took away from Teeter the night before. He didn't have a drop when he went home, but you brought him a bottle. Now I've got to know why."

"I see," Carney said. "I didn't think you'd ever squeeze me, Charlie. I thought you'd always remember what you owed me."

"I remember," Charlie said. "Do you think this is easy?"

Carney hesitated, then shook his head. "There's nothing lower on this earth than a man who'll abuse a good woman," Carney said. "Whatever pain I've caused Fred Teeter bears not the slightest on my conscience. The man got what he deserved."

"Who decides that? You?"

"Yes, me! Who has a better right?"

166

"I don't see that you have any right at all," Charlie said frankly.

"Well, what do you know anyway?" Carney snapped. "You spend fifteen years of your life in a lice-ridden hut on the reservation and the rest of it one army camp after another then sit there and tell me my rights." He laughed. "Charlie, the trouble with you is that you forget who you are."

"Who am I, Doc?"

"An educated Indian," Carney said flatly. "What the hell else?" He slapped himself on the chest. "I brought you to town, broke you free. There were people here who said it couldn't be done, and people here who fought me, but I could fight harder. I don't need any man to tell me whether I'm right or wrong. I do what I do and I need no man's approval."

"I sent Fred Teeter home with his boys," Charlie said.

"You can't do that."

"I've already done it. And you're going to call Paul Sessler on the phone and make a recommendation to him that the court order be rescinded."

"Why would I do that, Charlie?"

"Because I just told you to. Because you know me and know I'll open a crack in you if you don't." He uncrossed his legs and his manner became less casual. "And you know better than to think I'm bluffing."

Carney opened and closed his mouth several times as though he couldn't find the right words, and he waved his hands, then said, "But Teeter is a swine!" He took his dead cigar from his mouth and threw it away. "Damn it, Charlie, don't you believe in justice?" He turned and paced back and forth. "So few men get what they have coming, and here, right here, is a man who's reaping his harvest." He stopped pacing and went to the window again and spoke in a softer voice. "When I was a young man, Charlie, I went off to war. Cuba. It wasn't much of a war, compared to the one you fought, but I was gone a year and a half. Like most men, there was someone waiting for me; a man needs that when he's fighting a war. But when I came back, I found that she'd married another man. I suppose if it hadn't been for my widowed mother, I'd have gone on a real toot, but her health was poor and I had a practice to tend to." He shrugged. "The man was a pig, of course, and her life was hell. She died in childbirth. He got off scot-free, Charlie. No one blamed him at all. Hell, eight months later he remarried and moved away and it never touched him at all. He never had to pay, not one bit, for killing her."

The sun was down and grayness came into the room but Carney did not switch on the lights; he remained by the window, staring out. Charlie sat there, silent, waiting, and Carney went on: "As a doctor, I've seen much of this. Men who have no

168

respect for women. Thank God I've never been like that. My mother lingered on for many years and I was devoted to her. I would have been as devoted to Anna if she'd only waited. Women are weak, Charlie. It's up to a man to understand that and forgive them for it. She never loved him, I'm sure."

"That's a lie," Charlie said. "She loved him. Teeter's wife loved him."

The thought enraged Carney and he swung around. "What do you know? No woman could love a man who treated her that way!"

"She loved him," Charlie repeated. "She'd have lived in a hole in a ground if that's all he had and had her children in a hayfield if that had to be." He got up and walked over to Carney. "It's not Teeter you're getting back at, Doc. It's the man who married the girl who didn't wait, the man who got away, as you put it, without being punished." He reached out and tapped Carney on the chest. "You call Paul Sessler tonight."

"I may not do that," Carney said.

"You'll do that," Charlie Two-Moon said calmly. "You'll do that because you know me. And you get off Teeter's back and stay off." Then he stepped to the door and stood with his hand on the knob. "It's been nice for you all these years, pretending that you were the injured party, so injured that you never had to risk your damned pride and be jilted twice. Hell, do you think this

169

was some new experience?" He shook his head. "You've got to think your way clear on this, Doc. Do you understand? You can't do this to people."

"I thought you were my friend," Carney said.

"If I wasn't," Charlie said, "I'd have gone to Sessler myself."

"Do you think it's the act of friendship to force a man to bare the scars on his soul?" Carney asked. "Charlie, where's all the years between us? Don't they mean anything to you?"

"More than you think."

"Then show me what they mean," Carney invited. "Show me that people have been wrong when they've said you'd take what you could get from me and turn on me."

"Doc, I'm turning *to* you," Charlie said. "Can't you see that?"

"By coming here and telling me the things I've believed are lies?" He laughed. "Charlie, you can't do that to a man." He waved his hands then thrust them into his pockets. "Yes, yes, I was hard on Teeter. Cruel, perhaps. I admit that. When he first came to me with gonorrhea I realized that he'd infected his wife and it enraged me. I was—very rough in my treatment and I confess that I enjoyed seeing him suffer. God, man, he'd sinned!" He blew out a long breath. "I examined his wife and found her pregnant. Of course, at best, the child would probably be born blind. Can you imagine the hell, the torment I endured

170

in those months, knowing the outcome, dreading it, and helpless to change it in the least?" He shook his head. "Charlie, I swear to you, this is the first time I have ever revenged a good woman for her suffering. I don't know what made me do it. Perhaps it was brooding about it, the week-to-week contact with the patient; she became—well, almost as dear to me as the one I lost. I suffered, Charlie, and Fred Teeter did not. The innocent bore the pain and the guilty no pain at all. Now do you understand?"

"Yes," Charlie Two-Moon said, "but it doesn't change anything." He opened the door. "And, Doc, you're not innocent. None of us are."

He went slowly down the stairs, knowing that nothing would ever be the same between himself and this man, and it was a sad knowledge.

When he reached the street he found a group of men standing near Kerrick's car and they turned to him when he came up, each of them trying to talk louder and faster than the others. Jim Holbrook had come to town for supplies and let the word out that Teeter was alive and unharmed and the news had gone up and down the street.

Dan Samuels, a farmer west of the reservation said, "Charlie, it's a good thing you and Jim hung around when you did. What made you think Teeter hadn't run off?"

"He had no place to go," Charlie said. "A man's got to have a hole before he runs to it."

They allowed that this was certainly the truth. Another farmer said, "Hear you're doing well with rabbits, Charlie. How does a man get started in that business?"

"With a buck and a few does," Charlie said jokingly. "But I wouldn't just rush into it. There's more to it than meets the eye."

They all laughed and Samuels said, "Now, Charlie, don't try to discourage the competition. Hell, don't the rabbits run wild on the prairie?" He turned to the others and winked. "It don't seem like no big chore to me to let rabbits do in a cage what they do naturally out in the grass."

Another man thrust his voice into the talk. "How about selling us some breeding stock, Charlie? Give us a good price."

They were jokingly pushing for a deal and he knew it, yet he had to be honest with them. "You want to come out to the farm and I'll give you some breeding stock."

"No, no, we'll pay for 'em," Samuels said. "We're all men who pay as we go along." He laughed. "And we all heard of Indian giving."

"You suit yourself then," Charlie said and got in the car and backed out of the parking place. At the corner he made a U turn and drove on out of town.

It was a shame, he thought, that men didn't listen more; it would save them a lot of grief. He supposed being an Indian and having been assured for years that he was really an inferior person had taught him to listen because that was what inferior people were supposed to do best. This had taught him a lot, and the army had taught him a lot, about how to go by the book, how to use the experience of others to his best advantage.

The weather was turning off sunny and warm and he figured it was about time to start ordering his turkeys. There wasn't much left to do to the pens and he had laid in enough mash to carry him through the summer. With any kind of luck he figured to net twenty-eight hundred dollars at the end of the year, and that was better than anyone else in the county was going to do.

Martha Frank saw the headlights turn into the yard and opened the screen door as he came across the porch. He could smell the meal she had ready and he quickly put his arm around her and kissed her. She had a way of melting to him when he held her and when he let her go she stood back and laughed nervously. "We really hadn't ought to do that when we're alone," she said. "You know?"

"Yes," he said and stepped inside. "Smells good."

"Pie too," she said. "Joe's cleaning the rabbit hutches." She took his arm and turned him and looked into his eyes. "Charlie, what happened?"

"Teeter will get to keep the boys," he said.

"Carney will give on that." He took off his coat and hung it up and went to the sink to wash. She followed him.

"Charlie, how far did you have to go?"

"All the way," he said. "I didn't want to do it, not even for a friend, let alone Teeter. But it's got to end, Martha. Doc's got to see that."

"And suppose he doesn't?"

Charlie Two-Moon put his arm around her. "We'll figure that out when we come to it," he said. "A man's just got to swing at the ball as it comes over the plate."

"And now and then you get beaned," Martha said.

"I must show you my lumps," Charlie told her, then went to the door to call the boy.

15

The spring was a busy time of the year for Charlie Two-Moon. His turkeys arrived and he made his last shipment of rabbits and banked the check. Holbrook's crops were in and pushing through the black earth and it looked like a good year, for the rain was heavy and scattered, not the usual downpour that soaked everything for three days in a row then ran off in the gullies and creeks. The river behind Charlie's place came to a good level, but didn't break the banks.

Fred Teeter needed money and Charlie offered him a job, from six in the morning until two in the afternoon, and Teeter seemed glad to get it. It took some of the back-breaking work off Charlie Two-Moon and gave Teeter enough to buy materials to rebuild a small house.

It seemed to Charlie that a lot of farmers were going into the rabbit raising business; he'd sold fifty does and ten bucks and tried to offer them advice, but they all turned it down and swore they knew what they were doing. It amused him because he had observed that most men always swear to a thing when they are not at all sure.

He spent some time at the reservation, but

steered clear of his relatives although they came twice to his place to visit. Only it was to beg, and he knew it, and he always gave them something, not as much as they wanted, but enough to keep them from becoming angry.

They no longer tore down his fence or danced in his yard, and they left the children and the dogs at home; he had a firm rule about that because he didn't want them in the turkey pen or near the rabbits.

March came quicker than he thought it would, and on the day he was supposed to meet the train, he shaved carefully and put on a dark blue suit and his best white shirt. Martha came from the reservation the day before to make sure his spare rooms were in order and she cleaned the house from top to bottom although it really didn't need it.

And an hour before train time she drove into his yard with Jules Kerrick's car and they went to town together to wait at the depot. She wore an organdy dress and a bonnet that he thought very fetching and she tried not to be nervous.

"I haven't seen them for nearly three years," she said. "You'll like my father, Charlie."

"So you've said." They stood in the shade of the depot for the sun was warm, and he knew it was about train time for the baggage man wheeled up four of his iron-wheeled carts loaded with outgoing express packages.

There were a few people in the station and some outside and they drew glances, but that was all. Then they heard the train as it approached the river bridge and Martha said, "Charlie, hold my hand."

The engine rumbled into the station with its heat and noise and great weight that made the windows rattle and the ground tremble, then passed on to stop far down, like a runner breathing after a fast dash.

They walked along the line of passenger coaches, then Martha waved and they went forward as a tall, slender man with a shock of white hair helped a rather frail woman down to the cinder platform.

She went ahead and hugged them, then took her mother's arm and turned. "Mama, this is Charlie."

He wasn't really sure what he should do, offer to shake hands, or just stand there for he was conscious of his dark skin and dark hair and the fact that he was an Indian and would be until the day he died.

Mrs. Frank looked at him, then smiled and said, "Why, Charlie, you're a handsome devil," and she put her arms around him and he kissed her cheek.

Owen Frank shook hands and his grip was solid and he said, "Let's get our grips. Do we have far to go?"

"We've got a car," Martha said and walked with her mother.

Charlie and Owen Frank got the luggage and stowed it and Frank sat in the front while Charlie drove. As they passed through town, Owen Frank said, "I've always wanted to see this part of the country. The land along the river looks particularly good."

"It sets a man pretty much free of the rains," Charlie said. "Either that or have a good well, and you can't handle more than thirty acres with the best of wells."

Martha and her mother chatted in the back seat, but Charlie knew they were listening to everything that was being said; he could see their eyes in the rearview mirror, and womanlike, they could talk and listen at the same time; it was a gift denied men.

Owen Frank looked at both sides of the street when they stopped to let a truck cross. He saw the cars parked and the wagons and the horses that belonged to Indians from the reservation; they came in to shop and to look around and no one liked it, but they had government money every month and the merchants liked that.

The traffic cleared and Charlie started the car and went on down the street and he saw the crowd in front of Mel Allen's Pool Parlor, then Martha reached across the back seat and touched his shoulder. "Charlie, isn't that Tom Walks Far?"

Charlie could make it out in spite of the crowd of men; Allen was in his doorway, pushing Tom Walks Far, and George Grant, the constable was there and not doing much of anything. The rest of the men there were just crowd, not taking a part in this one way or another.

There was no parking place, so Charlie stopped the car in the street and opened the door. To Owen Frank and his wife he said, "I'm sorry. He's my cousin," and went around the front of the car and hauled men aside to get into the center of this thing.

Mel Allen saw him then and smiled. "Why, hello, there, Charlie. Didn't know you was in town." He looked at Tom Walks Far; there was a trace of blood in the corner of his mouth and his lower lip was puffed where he had been hit. "Nothin' to concern yourself about, Charlie. Just a little argument. You know I don't cheat anybody."

"Not if they catch you," Charlie said. He looked at George Grant. "What do you know about this?"

"Now, Charlie, don't get excited," Grant said. "I saw it all and the Indian accused Mel of shortchanging him."

Charlie Two-Moon took Tom by the arm. "Go on back to the reservation."

"He cheat me. I buy ten cigars. He cheat me."

179

"Get your cigars at the reservation store," Charlie said. "Won't you ever learn?"

"That's what I told him," Allen said hotly. "I don't need his damned business."

Charlie pointed his finger at him. "You shut your mouth because I wasn't talking to you." He looked at George Grant. "Why don't you do your job and get these people off the sidewalk?"

Mel Allen's temper flared. "Don't let him order you around, George. Use your authority if you have to."

"I'd like to settle this without further trouble," Grant said. "Indian, why don't you do like Charlie says and go back to the reservation?"

Charlie gave him a gentle shove. "Go on, Tom. Go on now." He stood there while Tom Walks Far went to his pony, flipped up and rode out, then he turned his attention to Mel Allen. "Did you hit him?"

"Hell yes, I hit him! Look now, Charlie, you're not talking to some guy on the street. I was born and raised in this town. My father—"

"Your father was a good man who left you half of main street, which you promptly pissed away until all you have left is this crummy pool hall," Charlie said. "Now if you don't want Indians in the place, then put up a sign: *Indians Keep Out*. And when you feel like hitting one, you come and see me and I'll stop whatever I'm doing and let you take a poke at me. But I'll poke back."

"Boy, you sure do like to hunt trouble," Allen said and laughed. "What do you want to pick a fight with me for?" He looked at George Grant. "Can't you get this crowd broken up? Come on now, fellas, clear the sidewalk." He was eager to have done with it now, and Charlie Two-Moon turned and walked out to the street where the car was parked. Mel Allen yelled, "I'll remember this, Charlie."

Without answering or looking back, Charlie got into the car and drove on down the street. Finally he said, "It's a shame your first impression has to be a bad one."

"What's bad about it?" Owen Frank asked. "You did what you thought was necessary, and I can't recall ever seeing a bunch backed down so neatly." He turned and looked at his daughter. "Seems that you're getting a real tom turkey."

"I hope this doesn't make an enemy for you," Mrs. Frank said.

"He was never a friend," Charlie admitted. "Tom ought not to have gone in there in the first place, but the trouble with the reservation Indians is that they just can't get it through their heads they're not wanted."

"I heard the conversation," Owen Frank said. "Do you think that man cheated your cousin?"

"I suppose he did," Charlie said. "Mel's not the most honest man I know." Then he shrugged. "But then, neither is Tom Walks Far. He'd steal

181

an extra cigar if he thought he wouldn't get caught at it."

"Excuse me for asking," Owen Frank said, "but I don't get the connection of your names. You're cousins, you say?"

"Well, not really," Charlie said. "Fact is, I don't know anything about my people, or what tribe I'm from. Back in '89, when I was three years old, there was an epidemic and the agency people moved me here and farmed me out to raise."

"There must have been some record."

"Yes, but there was a fire that winter and the headquarters burned down. Since I was born on the reservation and spoke no particular language, there was no way to tell. Jules Kerrick, the agent, thinks I'm Cherokee, you know, being tall and having a sharp nose and not quite as dark a skin as some of the others." He looked at Owen Frank and smiled. "But you couldn't prove it by me."

When they turned into Charlie's farm, Owen Frank said, "Well, now, a painted fence. Nice, Charlie. Very nice."

Joe Teel rushed out to meet the car and he was introduced, then insisted on carrying all the luggage into the house, and Martha went on in with her mother while Charlie and Owen Frank walked around the barnyard. Charlie was proud of his place, and what he had put into it and what he expected to get out of it, and Frank was impressed with the rabbits and turkeys.

"Never had much to do with poultry," he admitted. "But I guess there's money in it. And hard work."

"They take a lot of care," Charlie said. "They're prone to some diseases and once it starts, you've lost them all." He walked over to the well curbing and sat down and looked at Owen Frank. "I don't think I ought to beat around the bush with you, Mr. Frank. Martha's told you we want to get married. What do you think about it?"

"About you being an Indian?" He shrugged his thin shoulders. "Charlie, I always gave my daughter credit for having good sense. She was never one to rush into anything. So when she wrote me and told mother and me she'd fallen in love, I was willing to bet she'd found a good man." He took out a cigar for himself and offered one to Charlie, who took it and scratched a match on the curbing. "I don't expect a man to ask me permission before he does a thing, and I don't usually bother anyone else with mine. But you've asked me so I'll give you a straight answer. Charlie, if you love my girl and she loves you, marry her. Be happy. It's a short life at best, so make the most of it. Martha's grandmother got took by an Indian buck. It was rape, to be sure, but she got caught with a child. My father married that woman, Charlie, knowing she was carrying a child, and when one man ventured an opinion, my father whipped out his .44 and pistol-whipped him senseless. It takes guts to do what you want. From what I've seen so far, you're a man, and when it comes down to it, what the hell else is there to be?"

"I guess that answers my question," Charlie said. "But I didn't want you to think I was some reservation buck."

Owen Frank's pale eyes pulled into wrinkled squints. "What's wrong with that?"

"They rate pretty low around here," Charlie said.

"Why?"

"Because I guess they're content to be that way. I don't know. I wasn't."

"It's the difference that makes the world go around," Frank said. "This adopted cousin of yours, is he happy on the reservation?"

"I guess. He doesn't work much and he lives like a pig."

"Then why don't you stop worrying about him?"

Charlie raised his head quickly. "Is that what I'm doing?"

"Sure," Frank said. "Why did you stop the car and interfere? The truth is, Charlie, you feel that you'd somehow been insulted because he'd been. Let them get out and fight their own fights. You did."

Charlie Two-Moon puffed on his cigar. "I

hate to say it, but I wouldn't give you two whoops in hell for the whole lot on the reservation."

"That's not fair," Frank said. "Let a man be what he wants to be. Everytime you apologize for one of them, you're apologizing for yourself and you don't have to do that. I watched those men on the street, Charlie. Even the pool-hall owner respected you. Like you, no, but respect you he did. He pulled in his wire pretty damned fast when he found which way the ball was going." He reached out and slapped Charlie on the shoulder. "Let's go in the house before the women get suspicious."

Charlie went ahead and opened the screen door; Martha and her mother were in the parlor and Mrs. Frank said, "This is a lovely house, Charlie. And the trees give so much shade." She looked at her husband. "You were doing a lot of talking out there, Owen."

"Oh," he said, "just about ships and tacks and sealing wax."

Charlie Two-Moon glanced at Martha, then said, "We were talking about the Franks getting an Indian in the family."

"There's nothing new there," she said, looking steadily at Charlie, but smiling gently. "We're not a people who take alarm easy. You've got to give us credit for that."

"I've got a bit to learn," Charlie admitted,

185

embarrassed that he'd so bluntly introduced the subject.

Owen Frank said, "Man's first step toward knowledge is his admission of ignorance. Is there any coffee in this house?"

"Always," Martha said and went into the kitchen. Charlie waved Owen Frank into a chair and sat down. The sun was filtered by the curtains and the room was cool and quiet except for the chatter of birds outside. The turkeys were noisy but Charlie had the pens far enough away from the house so that it was just a faint background gabble.

He said, "I—ah wish I could guarantee Martha a life of rural peace, but I'm the kind of a man who just has to take sides in everything that comes along." He smiled and shook his head. "I guess you already figured that out, from what happened in town."

Elizabeth Frank fanned her face with a magazine. "Well thank goodness," she said. "I never could abide a wishy-washy man." She looked at Owen. "He proposed to me twice and I said maybe, then one day he stopped the buggy to thrash a man who was kicking a dog." She laughed. "He spent the weekend in jail for that, and I was waiting for him when he got out. We were married that afternoon."

"I'll be damned," Charlie said softly.

"My words exactly when I found her waiting

in the constable's office," Owen Frank said. "Ah, here's my coffee. Thank you, Martha." He filled his cup and leaned back in the chair. "I have a married son, you know, but so far they've had no children. Charlie, I hope you're not a man to put a thing like that off."

"Well now, I hadn't thought—that is, we hadn't talked about it." He looked at Martha and color came into his cheeks.

Then she laughed. "Here, Charlie, take your coffee. You look as though you're going to choke." She bent and poured and her eyes met his. "Charlie's thinking about it now, Papa."

"Oh, come on," Charlie said, then quickly lifted his cup.

16

Jules Kerrick drove over to Charlie Two-Moon's place on a Thursday afternoon, just a week after Tom Walks Far's trouble in town. He parked his car by the well and went to the house, and Elizabeth Frank invited him in and got him a glass of iced tea.

"The weather's turning off warm," Kerrick said, putting his hat on a small table. "Enjoying your stay?"

"I certainly am. The men are in the turkey yard. They likely saw you drive up and will come in. Sugar?"

"Thanks, no, I like it this way." He sipped his tea. "My wife extends an invitation to supper on Saturday night."

"Why, that's nice," Mrs. Frank said. She turned her head as the back door opened and closed and Charlie and her husband came in. Kerrick started to get up, but Frank waved him back and shook hands.

"Good to see you again. Is that tea?"

"I'll get some more glasses," Elizabeth said and went into the kitchen.

Charlie Two-Moon rolled a cigarette and said, "Isn't that your good suit, Jules?"

188

"Yes," Kerrick said. "I want to attend the meeting of the town board tonight, Charlie. Will you come with me?"

"Is there a reason why I should?"

"Yes. You're Indian."

Charlie waited until he had his glass of tea before saying anything. "What's on your mind, Jules?"

"It may be rather hard to explain," Kerrick said. "Charlie, I was never a brilliant student in college and when I got out, the only teaching job I could get was on the reservation. I was your teacher the last three years you were in the reservation school."

"You did all right by me," Charlie said.

"I really didn't," Kerrick said. "I was a poor teacher who taught only to save enough money to buy the job of resident agent. Yes, I gave four hundred dollars for that job, Charlie. A politician took my money and three months later the other agent was transferred, and I took over." He drank the rest of his tea and put the glass aside. "Since then I've paid out a few more hundred to stay."

"Well, I always knew there was some monkey business going on at the agencies," Charlie Two-Moon said, "but I know you cleaned out the petty crookedness, Jules. What are you trying to tell me, that I'm wrong?"

Kerrick shook his head. "I've done my best to cut out the graft, the cheating on weight of beef sold to the agency, the quality of the products sold at the store. And I've done a good job. But it's a hopeless, endlessly heartbreaking job, Charlie. God, you know what it's like. Out of that school there have only come two people who benefited. Really benefited. You and Joe Teel. The others just can't be reached at all."

"One at a time, two at a time, I guess that's the way it's got to be," Charlie said.

"Yes, that's the way it is and I've long ago accepted that. I've also accepted the fact that a large percentage of the town's income is derived from the reservation, from purchases made directly by me, and, from the government checks handed out each month. Charlie, for as long as I've been there, those Indians go to town with their eighteen dollars and seventy-five cents and they come home broke, carrying some trinket or a cheap blanket." He shook his finger. "The town's drawn its last blood from the reservation, Charlie. And I'm going to tell that to the council tonight."

"Jules, you haven't got a chance," Charlie said.

"Alone I haven't," he said softly. "But if I had help—"

"Don't mix me into it, Jules. I've left the reservation."

"They're your people, Charlie. If I close the reservation, what do you think the merchants in town will do?"

"Tear your throat out," Charlie said. "Or at least go to their politician friends and have you fired. If you, as agent, closed the reservation and wouldn't allow anyone off it, they'd claim it was a hardship, a personal thing." He shook his head. "Within ten days you'd get orders from Washington, orders you couldn't refuse to obey."

"But suppose the Indians refused to leave the reservation?"

"They wouldn't do that," Charlie said.

"But suppose they wouldn't."

He thought about it and shrugged. "The shoe would be on the other foot. Washington might want to know why. You'd get your chance to tell them. So would they. But you're dreaming, Jules."

"No, I'm not. Help me, Charlie. Help your people."

"Now wait a minute. What kind of influence do you think I have anyway?"

"Charlie, the very mannerisms and beliefs you dislike about your people becomes now the very thing, the only thing that will save them. For a week now I've heard the talk constantly, going through the reservation like a brush fire. Talk of Charlie Two-Moon who got out of his car and spoke to these men in town and made their faces go pale." He held up his hand so he could go on without interruption. "They talk of Charlie Two-Moon who changes the color of the wild rabbits

191

and makes them very fat and sells them for a lot of money. It's talk of Charlie who went to far lands to find his fortune, and Charlie the hero of the war. Their medicine man admits that he feels the ground tremble when you walk, and he has convinced them that you brought Fred Teeter back from death and walked on the hot ashes without getting burned."

"Aw, Jules, you know—"

"Yes, yes, *we* know. We know it's a hard fist and a strong right arm that makes men like Allen backpedal in a hurry. *We* know your rabbits are a far cry from the jacks that run wild. *We* know all these things, Charlie, but they don't want to believe the real story; they want to make up their own." He leaned forward. "Charlie, you're the leader of your people now. They will obey your word to the last child without question."

"You want me to speak for them?"

"Yes," Jules Kerrick said. "Tonight, at the council meeting."

"They won't believe me."

"They'll soon learn to believe you," Kerrick said.

Charlie looked at Owen and Elizabeth Frank; they were watching him. Then he said, "I never wanted to be the leader of anything."

"Sometimes we have no choice in these things," Kerrick said. "I'm going to be honest with you, Charlie. You've tried to push aside your Indian background and no one cared because it didn't hurt anybody. But if you turn your back on your people now, you're going to regret it as long as you live."

"It's you who's forcing the issue," Charlie said.

"Yes, because it has to be forced. You see that." He stood up. "Don't hedge with yourself, Charlie. Don't debate. What does your heart say?"

He stood there, rotating the ice in his glass, making it slide around, then he put it aside. "It'll take me a half hour to bathe and change my clothes, Jules."

Kerrick grabbed his hand and pulled him to him and hugged him briefly, then he turned away and sniffed his nose and Charlie went to his room.

Owen Frank said, "That didn't come cheap, Mr. Kerrick. He'll pay for this decision."

"He knows that." He turned and looked at Owen Frank. "But he's not afraid."

"I think he is," Frank said softly. "I think he's learned to live with it though."

They drove into town early and had supper at the hotel, and afterward they went to the Grange Hall where the council meetings were held and took seats near the front of the room where they could be seen.

Daniel Ricker was the mayor and presided over the meeting. Milo Mortenson sat on his right and he nodded civilly to Charlie Two-Moon when he happened to glance that way. Al Winkler was there, and Doctor Carney, and three other men who sat in their stiff collars and smoked cigars.

There was no crowd at all in the hall for these meetings were generally without vitality, routine affairs that began at eight and dismissed before nine.

Ricker called the meeting to order and had the minutes of the last meeting read, and very dryly they plowed through the old business and got it out of the way, hoping to adjourn and go home. When Ricker asked if there was any new business, he poised his gavel, expecting none, expecting to entertain a motion to call it quits. He held his gavel poised and his mouth slightly open as Jules Kerrick stood up.

"Mr. Mayor, gentlemen of the council. I have a matter to bring up before this body."

"Very well," Ricker said, brushing his mustache. "Make it brief. My wife's expecting me home early."

"Thank you," Kerrick said and opened his briefcase. "I have here the government audit of reservation expenditures for the last sixteen years, but to save time, I will refer only to the one last year, 1925. Gentlemen, the total budget ran to sixty-three thousand eight hundred dollars, and thirty-four cents. Of this amount, all, save staff salaries, was spent in this township. Add to that one hundred and ten thousand, four hundred

194

dollars in government checks for the four hundred and sixty adult Indians, and you have a pretty sizeable sum of money."

Milo Mortenson said, "Really, Kerrick, we're well aware of these figures."

"Indeed I'm sure you are, sir," Kerrick said. "The merchants have been swindling that amount from these uninformed people for some years."

There was an immediate uproar, shouted denials, and there was no one at the table who now believed he'd go home early. Ricker hammered for order and finally got it. He speared Kerrick with his eyes and said, "You've come here with some strong talk. Are you prepared to make charges against citizens of this town?"

"No, I'm not," Kerrick said.

Milo Mortenson laughed and said, "Then what's the idea stirring us up?"

"I don't think charges would achieve my purpose," Kerrick said. "Let me make my position clear. You do not want the Indians, or the reservation. Just the money. That's the way it's been for years."

"So?" Ricker said.

"So I think it's time to reverse the procedure. The reservation will remain where it is, but the money will no longer flow into your pockets."

"And how do you propose to stop it?" Mortenson asked.

Charlie Two-Moon spoke without getting up.

195

"I'll tell them not to come to town anymore."

They all laughed, except Oswald Carney; he watched Charlie's face and then held up his hand for silence, and got it. "What do you get out of this, Charlie?"

"A lot of trouble."

"That's for sure," Carney said. "All right, I'll rephrase the question. What do you think the reservation Indians are going to get out of this?"

"A fair shake in town."

Carney waved his hand. "These merchants make their own policy, Charlie. We can't dictate to them."

"Pass some ordinances then."

"Oh, stop the damned arguing," Mortenson said. "This is a bluff, pure and simple. He hasn't got any say over those Indians." He glanced at Kerrick. "And you can't push your way in here and threaten us into elevating those sixth-class citizens you ride herd on. I've lived around Indians all my life and I never knew one who didn't stink or turn savage when the chips were down. And there's a lot of men in town who agree with me, if they only had guts enough to admit it." He looked around at the men at the table, but none had a comment.

Ricker seemed in control of his temper. "Mr. Kerrick, this is a sudden—well, objection on your part. I don't believe you've ever made a complaint before."

"That's right. Because I couldn't do anything about it before."

"And you can now?" Carney asked. He laughed. "Kerrick, this town lives off Indian money. Try to cut that off and you might as well pack up and leave; we'll be getting a new agent."

"He can't cut it off, I tell you," Mortenson said heavily. "Hell, I know these Indians. They're like children. They won't do as he tells them. They never have."

Again Ricker spoke softly. "Mr. Kerrick, let us look into this matter and recommend at next month's meeting a reasonable solution."

"I'm offering a solution," Kerrick said, "but you gentlemen seem loathe to accept it."

"You call this a solution?" Al Winkler snapped. "You don't have the authority to keep these Indians out of town."

"*I* don't intend to," Jules Kerrick said pleasantly. "And gentlemen, you don't have the authority to *make* them spend their money here either."

"This is going in a circle," Ricker said. "Mr. Kerrick, will you give us a month?"

"No," Kerrick said.

Doctor Carney raised his hand. "Jules, when is this mass boycott going to commence?"

"It has begun," Kerrick said and closed his briefcase. He turned to the door and Charlie followed him and in the hall Carney caught up with them. He looked from one to the other, his expression puzzled.

"Jules, this could hurt your career," he said.

"What career? You'll have to do better than that, Carney."

"All right then, if you don't have sense enough to listen." He turned to Charlie Two-Moon. "You've cut out a good life for yourself. Did it the hard way and people respect you for it. Hell, give them another ten years and they'll forget you're an Indian."

"I once thought that was a wonderful thing," Charlie said. "Now I've changed my mind. I don't want them to forget it."

"Well, now you're going about it in exactly the right way," Carney said. "Get these people down on you, Charlie, and you might as well pack up and leave." He shook his head. "Are you doing this because of me, Charlie?"

"No, I'm doing it for my people."

Carney snorted in disgust. "God, I thought you learned better. Hell, you don't belong to any of them."

"A man belongs whether he wants to or not," Charlie said. "Back clear of this, Doc."

"I can't."

"Neither can I," Charlie said and went out with Jules Kerrick.

17

Jules Kerrick made the arrangements by returning to the reservation and merely telling the first Indian he saw that Charlie Two-Moon was coming in the morning to speak to all of his people; there would be no more to do for the word would make the rounds by nightfall and they would come from the vast corners of the reservation.

Charlie Two-Moon kept Joe Teel out of school so the boy could go to the reservation with him, and they arrived just after breakfast and Jules Kerrick met them on the porch.

"Why don't you help Martha with school?" Kerrick asked the boy. "She's always needed an assistant."

"Would that be permitted?" Joe Teel asked.

"Yes," Kerrick said. "You go ahead." The boy ran off, and he looked after him for a moment, then said, "It'll be good for the pupils. They'll go home with stories of how well Joe is doing and someday one of them may remember it and get off this place." He sighed. "Such a very big, important problem and we have to chip away from it one at a time, one or two a generation. A very slow way, Charlie." He brought out cigars and offered one. "But I've always been of the opinion that the Indians are driven here. They look outside and it turns them back to their huts and their sheep, for they're convinced that poverty and filth and ignorance is better than the trouble they'd find off the place." He looked at Charlie. "We've got to change that. It won't do to wait longer, Charlie."

"Running out of time or patience, Jules?"

"It would be closer to the truth to say that I had to wait for the messiah, Charlie. I'm a white man, a stranger. No matter how long I'm here, I'll never be one of them. There's that wall between us." He stood on the porch, looking at the large yard, and the Indians began to gather, about a hundred in a loose crowd, but more were coming, some riding, many walking; they were coming from four directions. "There's five languages spoken here, and a dozen dialects. The young speak English. The old, well, they don't want to speak it. Yet there is not an adult here who does not understand it." He looked at Charlie Two-Moon. "It took Moses to lead his people out of Egypt, didn't it?"

"He was considerably older," Charlie said. "I didn't sleep much last night, thinking about this. You're pulling me back, Jules, but how can I help myself?" He puffed on his cigar and searched for words. "Getting off the reservation didn't free me of anything, did it, Jules?"

"It didn't change your skin," Kerrick said. "But you're free, Charlie, only you don't know it. Let me put it another way if I may. A man has to be *of* something. Do you understand what I mean? A man has to be of German extraction, or of Swedish, or of Indian, or of this family, or of this town, or of that country. Every man stands for something past. He doesn't begin a life at fifteen and believe there was nothing before." He studied the jammed throng in the yard. "When you talk to them, Charlie, remember who they are. Remember who you are."

Charlie Two-Moon wondered how he would quiet them so he could speak, then he found that when he stepped forward to the porch edge, a hush fell, and he could not recall ever having heard the reservation so quiet. No dogs barked. No children laughed and screamed in play. No infant wailed.

He said, "Is there anyone among you who does not know me?" And it was a strange feeling to look at that sea of impassive faces and find that they all knew him when he could not have called fifty by name. Yet it was like looking into a many-sided mirror reflecting himself, and he knew what he would say, how he would speak to them. "Will my uncle, Ed Lame Bear, and my cousin, Tom Walks Far, honor me by standing at my side."

It was the thing to do, something he did not

have to do, and he knew what effect it would have, and afterward both men would be held in high respect because he was sharing the honor of his name with them.

Both men came to the porch and Charlie took off his coat and put it around the shoulders of Ed Lame Bear and a shout rose, filling the yard, for this was a gift in view of all; it was an embrace, a kiss, an acknowledgment of family. Charlie took off his hat and placed it on Tom Walks Far's head and again there was shouting and arm-waving and both these men stood together, behind Charlie Two-Moon, who began to speak.

He knew how to talk to them, what to say to them, for their ways were not gone from his mind at all, merely pushed back by the manner of his living. It was the Indian way to boast and he told of the many things he had done and the places he had been and it was his childhood again where he had spent long nights listening to old men tell of the days of their youth, the days of their fathers when the buffalo herds roamed the prairie and the white men lived in fear.

He made it around to his point and motioned for Tom Walks Far to step forward, and he told them all again of what had happened in town and they were angry about that, as they had always been angry when they were cheated and pushed around and their women insulted.

It wouldn't do to talk about money with

these people; they really had a poor concept of economy and could not see any merit at all in saving. When they had it they spent it and when they were broke they waited patiently until the next check came. So he went back to the old way, to the medicine talk.

After Tom Walks Far had been struck on the mouth, Charlie Two-Moon had a vision, and from the nodding heads he knew he was getting to them. The vision was clear. What he must command them to do was clear.

They were not to leave the reservation and go into the town for any reason.

He would speak for them, act for them, and he would come again, to tell them when it was all right to leave the reservation. He made a sweeping motion with his hand. "You have heard me speak," he said, and turned and went inside the building.

From the window in Kerrick's office he watched the crowd break up, then Kerrick came in and closed the door. "They'll do what you say, Charlie. Thanks."

He looked at Kerrick and said, "Standing out there, playing to all their beliefs and omens, it was as though I had never left this place at all. It seemed that my life away from here was simply an interlude until I came back. Hail the American Indian." He looked at his dead cigar butt and decided it was too short to light and dropped it in

Kerrick's wastebasket. "I'm going home and wait for the fireworks to start. How long do you think it will take?"

"A week," Kerrick said. "Tomorrow, when there are no Indians in town, they'll think it's a coincidence. The next day they're going to wonder and on the third day they'll start to talk. I give it a week."

Charlie nodded. "And what do you think we'll really win, Jules?"

"Probably nothing, but we've got to try."

"I guess," Charlie said, turning to the door. "Do you suppose Martha could bring the boy home?"

"Yes, I'll tell her. You go on."

Charlie mounted his horse and rode toward his place, in no hurry, yet holding to a steady pace. It wasn't good to push something at another man, and the anger the merchants would have would be real and justified. Yet Charlie knew that the Indians had a right to be angry, and what it boiled down to was whether these third-class citizens were going to be raised to second class or not.

He had no illusions about what this would probably cost him. His place in the community, what acceptance he had, was dollars and cents acceptance. If he hadn't had cash in hand he would have been expected to go to the reservation and herd sheep like the others. But he'd had cash and he got a white man's haircut every month and didn't wear silver belt buckles and bright shirts and people kind of passed over him, left him alone.

Only he knew they really hadn't. He was a smart Indian making a go of it and a lot of men were waiting for him to have his hard luck, and when it happened they wouldn't feel sorry or care. Some would. Some always cared, and he had his friends; he knew that and appreciated it but he'd always be Charlie Two-Moon, that Indian who bought the Robins place.

He put up his horse and found Owen Frank in the turkey yard, finishing up with the feeding. Frank put aside his pail and came over. "Where's the boy?"

"Martha will bring him back," Charlie said.

Frank nodded. "You look like a man with doubts, Charlie."

"I have them," he admitted. "Under the circumstances, it's reasonable. I've just taken up sides, Owen, which is something I promised myself a long time ago not to do."

"Every man's got to declare himself sooner or later," Frank said. "Come on in. Elizabeth baked a pie."

Jules Kerrick was a bit off on his prediction; four days went by and on that afternoon, Milo Mortenson drove out from town and brought his brother and Doctor Carney with him. As they parked in the yard, Charlie walked out of the house and put his foot on the running board. "I've been expecting someone," Charlie said. "Are you the delegation?"

"You want to get right down to business?" Carney asked.

"Why not? Do you want to stand and say it or sit and say it?"

"There's no need to get out of the car," Milo Mortenson said. "Charlie, I thought you were bluffing."

"You should have known better," Charlie said. "Doc knew better."

"There are times," Carney said, smiling, "when people don't listen to me. This was one of them."

Mortenson gave him an irritated glance, then said, "Charlie, you've proved you could do it. Now let's call it off."

"Am I to think that you gentlemen have a deal for me?" Charlie asked.

"We have a proposition," Milo said. He nudged his brother. "Tell him about it, Austin."

"Charlie, we can understand your indignation, and Kerrick's, but we think this is the wrong way to get the job done."

Milo snapped. "Never mind the preliminaries, Austin. Tell him straight out."

Austin Mortenson bit his lip, then said, "Charlie, the school board had a meeting and they've decided that Joe Teel is a disrupting influence, and the school is crowded. They've voted to drop him at the end of this term."

"His grades are good," Charlie said. "He's been in one fight that I know of. Is this the only way you could figure to hit back?"

"You started this power play," Milo said. "Don't try to wipe it off on us."

Charlie looked at Oswald Carney. "How did you vote at the school board meeting? Or shouldn't I ask?"

"I voted to boot him out," Carney said frankly. He studied Charlie Two-Moon. "You go ahead and be a brave leader; so what does it cost you? Nothing?" He shook his head. "Don't be a fool, Charlie. You can't beat the drum and make a big noise without getting involved."

Charlie looked at Austin Mortenson. "Do you say the school is crowded, Austin?"

"Yes."

"Then you're a liar," Charlie said. "And the boy a disrupting influence?" Austin Mortenson nodded again. "That's another lie and you know it."

"We know it," Milo said impatiently. "But we can make it stick. Charlie, do you want to see that boy go back to the reservation and herd sheep?"

"You know the answer to that."

"Then get off our backs," Carney said pleasantly.

"What do you get out of this?" Charlie asked. "You don't treat Indians."

"No, but Indian money spread around goes far enough so that people I do treat do pay their bills." He leaned his arm on the edge of the window. "Charlie, you wanted to break away. All right, you did it. Now you're willing to put it on the block? Hell, they're not going to thank you for it. What do you want out of the town anyway? Thirteen doughnuts to a dozen for the Indians?"

"They deserve fair play," Charlie said. "This idea of jacking the price and selling them stuff they don't want has got to stop."

"Oh, hell," Milo Mortenson said, "I thought you'd been around a little. Do you think the Indians are the only ones who get taken to the cleaners? Hell, there isn't a merchant in town who hasn't put one over on me." He smiled. "When you bought the farm, I'd have sold it for three hundred less if you'd pushed a hard deal. So I snookered you out of three hundred dollars. Let the buyer beware; that's the first principle of law. If you want these Indians to keep from losing the buttons off their pants, then teach them what buttons are."

"Clean up your town or close the Indians out," Charlie said. "You may not like the terms, but that's what they are."

"What do you consider a clean town?" Milo asked. "You want a few ordinances on the books making it a crime to clean an Indian?" He laughed. "Mister, you tell Kerrick he's dreaming. For God's sake, you're hammering at man's last frontier when you kick his prejudices." His expression became serious, almost grim. "You do what you want, Charlie, but you're going to shoot this Teel boy's chances right in the ass."

"We want the answer now," Carney said. "No mamby-pamby. Straight out, Charlie."

"Well, I've worked hard trying to be a white man, and I don't think I ever really believed I'd make it. Joe Teel's an Indian, and we're talking about his people. His and mine." He stepped back from the car, and smiled. "We'll find another school."

"Not in this county," Milo said and started the car, his manner angry.

Then his brother leaned across him and said, "Charlie, take a week."

"God damnit, I told you no bargaining!" Milo said and jammed the car in gear and drove out. After they turned onto the road, Charlie Two-Moon went back in the house.

18

Milo Mortenson waited on the steps in front of the schoolhouse. He stood to one side so that others could go on in, and when Doctor Carney arrived, Mortenson motioned for him to come over. "I told Paul Sessler I'd meet him here at a quarter after seven," Mortenson said. "What time is it?"

"About that," Carney said. "Milo, you told me this was going to be a private meeting. Do you need the school auditorium for that?"

"Private to the citizens of the town," Mortenson said. "We need organization, and we'll get it." He studied a car that drove up and parked, and when Jules Kerrick and Charlie Two-Moon got out, he swore under his breath. "How in hell did they find out?"

"I called them," Carney said matter-of-factly.

Mortenson looked angry enough to fight, but he choked it back. "Carney, I'm going to ask you why, and the answer had better be good."

"I'm not going to give you a reason," he said, then smiled as Kerrick and Charlie Two-Moon approached the step. He shook hands with both and said, "A little short notice but I'm glad you could make it."

"Wouldn't have missed it," Kerrick said. He glanced at Mortenson. "How's business?"

"It'll come back," Mortenson said. "Kerrick, this town will not knuckle under to pressure politics." He looked past them. "Ah, here's Sessler now. If you'll excuse me?" He left them and walked out to meet the county attorney.

"He's loving every minute of it," Carney said. "It would surprise me if he didn't run for public office next election." He looked at Charlie. "You'd run against him, of course."

"I couldn't run for dog catcher and win," Charlie said.

"My boy," Carney said, "you don't understand politics at all."

"Do I have to?" Charlie asked.

"Well, a lot of people are talking about you, Charlie. Good or bad, it's still talk." He took Charlie Two-Moon by the arm. "Would you excuse us a moment, Jules?" He pulled Charlie to one side and they leaned against the stone step railing, out of the traffic, where they could talk privately. "How's Fred Teeter getting along?"

"Fine," Charlie said. "He stays sober."

Carney scratched his chin. "Charlie, I got drunk the other night. I don't do things like that, you know, but I had to let go or explode. I want to make it up to Teeter."

Charlie shook his head. "You have to do better than that, Doc. You can't hurt a man then

211

pay it off that easy. You ought to know that."

"What do you want, a maudlin confession?" He blew out a long breath. "Charlie, you know, I think I can forget her now. After all these years I think she can rest in her grave where she belongs. It's funny how the truth can come to a man when he's drunk, the truth he's evaded all through his sober years. Charlie, I'm responsible for Teeter's fire. When I left his place I threw away a cigar butt. I'm sure it landed in some litter he'd swept out, caught and moved to the house. I saw the smoke as I was driving to the reservation but I kept on going. Afterward, well, you know about afterward."

"Doc, you could be liable for criminal prosecution."

Carney nodded. "I intend to talk to Sessler about it before he goes back to the county seat. But I want to make it up to Fred Teeter." He reached in his pocket and handed Charlie Two-Moon a bank draft. "Three thousand should rebuild everything he lost."

"Everything?"

"All right, just the buildings then." He studied Charlie Two-Moon. "Do you want me to draw a little blood too?"

"No," Charlie said. "I guess this is as sorry as you're going to be. I'm just beginning to understand that people are not always properly regretful for the things they do. It's another

212

bargain to them, a bargain they expect to make as cheaply as possible. But you're going to have to give Teeter the check yourself, Doc. He's coming in with Jim Holbrook. You can see him then."

"I see," Carney said. "You'd make me do that?"

"You're damned right," Charlie said. "Let's go inside."

They took seats near the back; Kerrick had saved two. Milo Mortenson occupied the speaker's platform, and he held up his hands for silence.

"Gentlemen, this meeting has been called to discuss a serious problem, and I've invited the county attorney, Mr. Sessler, to come here and advise us of our legal rights." He motioned to Sessler. "He will answer any questions you have, and then we'll discuss the situation. Mr. Sessler."

Sessler got up and adjusted his glasses and opened his briefcase. He had a professional manner, and as an elected officer of the county he knew how to make an impression. "Mr. Mortenson has given me all of the details, from his point of view, and I've studied this matter. Mr. Mortenson has also informed me of the steps already taken, and I would like to say now that I consider them all wrong; they should be rectified at the earliest opportunity." This pulled a gasp and a lot of murmuring out of the audience, but they fell silent when Sessler held up his hand. "Gentlemen, may I remind you that the Indian reservation is government property, administered by officials of the United States Government. The Indians living on that reservation are wards of the government as well as citizens of the United States. Now on this point, you must be clear. There is no equivocation, no debate, no question."

A man in the audience reared up. "Are you telling us they're better than we are?"

"No," Sessler said calmly. "I am merely saying that in the eyes of the law they are under the same protection of law that you are. As a ward of the government, they are—to use a simile—like minor children; their parents are responsible, and since each of you is a part of the government, you are responsible."

"The hell I am," the man said and sat down.

Sessler did not take up the argument. "The crux of this matter is that the Indians, through some agreement, no longer patronize the merchants and therefore deprive them of accustomed revenues. Mr. Mortenson has asked me to investigate the legal steps which we might take to restore this economic balance to the community." He paused and looked at the audience. "It's unfortunate that no representatives of the Indians is present, but—"

Charlie Two-Moon and Jules Kerrick got to their feet and Kerrick said, "We're here, Mr. Sessler."

Every head turned and angry mumblings filled the auditorium, but Sessler rapped the podium with his knuckles and they grew silent.

"If you'll step forward," Sessler said, "we can discuss this."

"To hell with them," a man shouted. "You tell us what we can do. That's what you're here for."

"That's right," another shouted. "We've heard what the Indians want, and we don't buy it."

Sessler held up his hands. "All right. Everyone calm down." He smiled. "I would like to call your attention to the fact that this anger will get you nowhere. Mr. Mortenson and a committee of men want to have Mr. Kerrick removed from his post. Gentlemen, I'm afraid that is an impossibility. He is appointed by the government and they do not remove men without due cause, or a complete investigation. As for due cause—"

"Ain't we got cause enough?" a man asked. "He's takin' food out of our mouths. Two more months of this and some of us will be out of business."

Paul Sessler was beginning to show an irritation. His voice took on a firmer note. "Gentlemen, you invited me here for a legal opinion, not to be your whipping boy. All right, I'm going to give you a legal opinion and you can like it or not. The last thing you want is an investigation by the government. For fifty years people have been getting fat off the Indians. Where there's a reservation, there are merchants with two kinds of merchandise, one for their white customers, and another for the Indians. Don't sit there on your sanctimonious—posteriors—and tell me this is a surprise to you. You buy the cheapest, gaudiest blankets you can, from people who manufacture them for this sole purpose, and mark them up 400 percent and peddle them to an ignorant squaw because she doesn't have sense enough to buy a brown blanket just because it's warmer. I could point my finger right now at thirty men who have been selling junk for years. You've paid for your homes with the profits, sent your kids to school and bought automobiles, and stuffed money in the bank. So you want a government investigation? You'd better pray that the newspapers don't play this up and bring one down around your ears because you haven't got a leg to stand on." He looked at them and let the stunned silence run for a moment. "If ever I saw men backing a busted flush, you're backing one here. Now I'm going to give you one last piece of advice: invite Jules Kerrick and Charlie Two-Moon up here, right now, and talk this out. If you don't settle this, I think you're through."

He went over to his chair and sat down, and some of the men got up and began to shout, but generally they agreed that Sessler made sense and they grew quiet. Pete Scarbrough stood up and said, "I want to make a deal. Damn it, I hurt and I'm not too proud to admit it."

This pretty much summed up their feeling, and Kerrick nudged Charlie and said, "All right, let's talk. It's time now." They got up and walked down the aisle and stepped onto the stage.

One of the men in the audience stood up and said, "I've got a question I want to ask you, Kerrick. If this is such an all-fired scratch in your craw, how come you haven't done anything about it before?"

"The Indians never had a leader," Kerrick said frankly. "As agent, I can do my best for them, but I still can't tell them what to think. To do that, a man would have to have their complete faith and trust. And most important, he would have to be one of them."

The man remained on his feet. "Then you didn't tell them to stay away from town?"

"No," Kerrick said. "They wouldn't have obeyed me. I've told them for years that they were being cheated, but it did no good."

"I told them to stay away," Charlie Two-Moon said. "And they'll stay away until I tell them different." He looked at the man still standing. "You want to ask me a question, Lillis?"

"I guess not," the man said.

"Don't sit down, Lillis!" It came out like the end of the whip and the man jumped slightly. Charlie Two-Moon walked to the edge of the stage and drilled the man with his eyes. "I want to tell you something, Lillis. I've considered you to be about as worthless a man as I've seen in this town. You've got a hole-in-the-wall store full of glass beads and baubles that you know an Indian woman can't resist, and the money they ought to spend on other things you put in your pocket because they've got to have trinkets around their neck."

"I can't help it if they're savages," Lillis said.

"The trouble is, you know their weakness, but they don't understand yours at all," Charlie said. "Sit down now, Lillis. People are tired of looking at you."

He sat down obediently and Charlie Two-Moon stood there, swinging his head from side to side, looking at all of them. "Mr. Kerrick has prepared a formal offer, which he'll read to you. But I'd like to boil down the terms in a language you can understand." He pointed to Pete Scarbrough. "Clean out all the junk knives and tools from your showcase, Pete. Sell one quality of merchandise." He swung his finger to another man. "Daniels, no more blue work shirts dyed red and green and sold for three times the price. Get rid of your cheap blankets and shoes with cardboard soles. You understand?"

Scarbrough stood up. "All right, Charlie, we see the point. But damn it, you've hit us hard."

218

"Tell me another way then."

Scarbrough shook his head. "It's that we don't like to be told we've got to do something, that's all."

"You suit yourself about what you do," Charlie said. "You'll just have to learn to get by on less profit."

Another man stood up. "Suppose we do what you want? What's to keep us from—well, sliding back to the way things were?"

"I can tell you about that," Jules Kerrick said. "A tribal council will be organized. This organization will have the power to control the Indians, and to arbitrate civic matters with your legally constituted city government. Gentlemen, if the tribal council finds anyone slipping back into their old ways, they can take the proper steps to correct it."

"I'm not going to be run by Indians," one man said.

Kerrick was undisturbed. "I don't care to debate it." He took out copies of his prepared statement. "I'm going to leave these with your city officials. And I want to leave you with something else. Times have changed. You've got to change with it. The Indians have to change too, and I believe they will. Clean up your town and the tribal council will clean up the reservation. Wash your town and we'll wash our Indians. Educate yourselves and we'll educate ourselves."

He looked at Milo Mortenson. "You can call me when you make a decision."

He closed his briefcase and stepped down, and Charlie Two-Moon followed him down the aisle. When they reached the lobby door they found Martha Frank standing there with her parents and Fred Teeter. Jim Holbrook was standing slightly behind them, half hidden.

"Let's get something to eat," Kerrick said. "I was too nervous to eat my supper." Then he looked around. "Didn't my wife come in?"

Martha laughed. "She's at the hotel. Too nervous to watch, I guess."

They left the school grounds and walked along a quiet side street. Fred Teeter said, "Charlie, you made a strong argument. I thought Lillis was going to bust. There weren't ten men in the place who didn't share your opinion, but none had ever expressed it before."

Martha held on to Charlie's arm, and he looked at her. "Quiet, aren't you?"

"You're letting them go too easily. Jules should have said something about the school."

"It'll be worked out," Charlie said softly. "In time."

"Regrets, Charlie?"

"Well, I wasn't the most popular man in town tonight," he said. "It's hard to give up something you've worked a long time for. I'm not a man who can live without the respect of other people,

Martha. Call it false pride or anything you want. Call it wrong for me, an Indian, to work hard just to overcome the background of my blood. It must be peculiar to you—it surely is with me—to offer it up for the people I tried to put behind me."

"I told you once that the greatest thing you could do would be to reach back," she said. "Such a good thing, Charlie, can never be bad."

He smiled at her. "I'll try to remember that."

19

The best meal the hotel served was the pot roast and they ordered that and tried to steer the talk away from useless speculation of what the outcome of the meeting might be. Kerrick hoped that a decision would be reached before they left town, but Charlie Two-Moon didn't think so, and Owen Frank agreed.

"Jules, it's a big thing, and people are afraid of big things. There'll be doubts as to whether they can do it, and you can do it," Frank said. "Give them time. You've made the push. It's up to them."

"He's right," Holbrook said. "Be patient, Jules."

Kerrick smiled. "Difficult, I assure you. For a good many years I've had to be satisfied that a poor job was my best effort. Now that there's some hope—" He shrugged and cut into his pie.

George Grant, the constable, came into the dining room and approached their table. He said, "Charlie, there's trouble making up over at Mel Allen's place." His glance to the ladies was apologetic. "Mel came back from the meeting pretty steamed up." He licked his lips. "Charlie, he says that if you want to find out just how he treats Indians, to come on over." Then he put out a hand and touched Charlie's shoulder. "Look now, I wouldn't take him up on that. He's got a good half dozen no-accounts in there with a batch of sawed-off cues. It's just Mel's big mouth shootin' off."

"Then why did you come and tell me?" Charlie asked.

Grant shifted his feet. "Well, I figured, when you didn't show, Mel might take it in his head to jump you on the street, and I didn't want you to be surprised."

Jim Holbrook said, "George, you sure don't like trouble, do you?"

"For a fact, I don't," Grant admitted. "Afterward I get sick at my stomach."

"Well, you're going to have it tonight," Holbrook said. "I'm with you, Charlie." He slid back his chair.

"Count me in," Teeter said.

Jules Kerrick sighed. "I'm a man of peace, but I used to box on the old school team." He laid aside his napkin, and George Grant stood there with wide eyes.

Elizabeth Frank said, "Owen, you let me hold those gold cuff links. I gave them to you twenty years ago and I'm not going to have you losing them on a pool-hall floor."

"You are," Frank said, handing her the cuff links, "the fairest rose in Texas."

George Grant backed up. "I'm going to get help." He turned and dashed out of the dining room and Charlie Two-Moon laughed.

Without a word he walked to the door and the four men followed him out and across the street. He pushed open the door of Mel Allen's place and they stopped just inside, and Allen was at one of the rear tables and he looked surprised. He had five men with him and they stood in one close-packed group.

Charlie Two-Moon raised a foot, put it against Allen's long showcase and with one heave sent it toppling with a splintering crash of glass that could be heard a half a block. When the last sliver tinkled down, Charlie said, "I understand you want trouble, Mel. You've got it."

Allen looked at the wreckage and said, "What's the matter, Charlie? Didn't you have guts enough to come alone?"

Owen Frank stepped farther down the narrow room and the others moved with him, splitting, going down on both sides of the table and when Frank reached the first one he picked up a cue. When he came to a wall rack full of cues he reached out and with the tip snapped them all free and they clattered and rolled on the floor around the feet of Mel Allen's friends.

Jim Holbrook laughed and did the same on

the other side of the room and hoped that these friends of Allen's would move; he'd like to see them make it across the scattered cues without falling down.

Owen Frank said, "He's alone now, mister."

Mel Allen looked at his friends, sealed off as well as if a wall had been shoved up, and if they made it across the cues, they had to lick four men who looked as though they'd be hard to lick. He licked his lips and said, "I ought to have you arrested, coming in my place and busting it up."

"You invited me," Charlie said. "Show me how you treat Indians, Mel?" He stood there, waiting, then smiled. "No? Not mad enough yet?"

Casually he moved to a pool table, picked up a cue and ripped the cushion. Allen looked at the torn cloth and swallowed hard. Then Charlie asked, "All you do is talk, is that it?" He went up to the man and Allen's fear got the best of him; he swung and bounced a fist off Charlie's cheekbone, cutting him, but not stopping him.

In close now, Charlie grabbed him, squeezed him, hurt him, and got behind him and grabbed him by the face, a hand over his nose and the other pulling at Allen's chin, and with Allen straining at Charlie's wrists, he was dragged to the wall mirror by the cigar counter.

There, Charlie pulled Allen's mouth agape and forced him to look at himself. "See?" Charlie said, shoving his face close. "See your big mouth? Look at your great big mouth."

Tears of pain ran down Allen's cheeks and he groaned and twisted and tried to break free, but Charlie Two-Moon held him and then he turned Allen around and with one hand he held him by the face, the fingers sunk deep into Allen's flesh under the cheekbones.

"Your mouth can get you hurt," Charlie said softly. "Are you so stupid you can't see that? God, man, I soldiered six years to buy a place where I wouldn't have to live like an Indian. Six years, you stupid man. Six years so I could live, thinking I'd be as good as white trash like you. But I've thrown that away for my people and I'm not sure yet whether I was right in doing that, or whether it was worth it. There are things in my mind that are like the raw end of a sore, stupid man, so don't prod me. Don't make noises at me with your big mouth. Do you think you can understand that?"

Mel Allen's eyes remained round and distended and he managed to nod his head, and then Charlie Two-Moon shoved against his face, and he reeled back and collided with one of the pool tables and he clung to it for support because his legs were weak. Then he looked past Charlie Two-Moon and said, "Grant, I want him arrested!"

"Go to hell," Grant said calmly and put his hands in his pockets.

Charlie turned and found Paul Sessler standing there with the constable. Oswald Carney stood behind them and a little to one side, and Sessler nodded to the damage. "Did you do that, Charlie? You can go to jail for it, you know."

Allen yelled, "Damn it, arrest him! What kind of a cop are you, Grant?"

"Do you want to sign a complaint?" Sessler asked. He looked at George Grant. "If he does, you'll have to arrest Charlie."

Grant slowly took his hands out of his pockets and unpinned his badge and threw it in the smashed showcase. "Get someone else. I never liked the job anyway. If a man hasn't got a right to defend his good name, then this is one hell of a country." He pointed to Mel Allen. "You invited Charlie over here to knock his head off with a pool cue."

"That's a lie!" Allen snapped.

Owen Frank jabbed one of Allen's friends in the stomach with the butt of the cue he still carried. "What do you say about that? I like a straight answer."

The warning was there and the man understood it; he nodded and said, "That's the gist of Mel's invitation, mister."

Allen said something under his breath, then looked at Paul Sessler and Carney. "Who the hell's side are you on anyway?"

"Not yours," Carney said.

Sessler said, "Charlie, the upshot of the meeting was to go along with your new tribal council. It wouldn't be any surprise to me if they put you on the town board. Mortenson was talking it up." He looked at Mel Allen. "Why don't you clean up this joint?" He turned to the wrecked cigar counter and dug about until he found a brand he liked. After he got it going, he said, "Your job's not going to be easy, Charlie; there are a lot of men like Allen here who can't see anything past their nose. But you don't take care of it like this, you hear?" His glance touched Frank and Kerrick and the others. "You men ought to know better than to get mixed up in this."

"How the hell do you stay out of it?" Holbrook asked.

Paul Sessler smiled. "A good question. The answer may not be easy."

"You may not be through with me yet," Mel Allen said. "I've got friends."

Sessler lifted an eyebrow. "Like those five? Allen, let me tell you something and hope it soaks into your thick skull. You have a business license, and you renew it each year. Now you don't automatically have that coming; it isn't something we just hand out." He waved his hand, and added, "Like I said: Clean out this joint and do a real good job of it." Then he turned and walked outside. George Grant and Doctor Carney followed him and a moment later

Charlie Two-Moon and the others stepped out.

Owen Frank said, "I'm going back to the hotel. You gents like to come along?" He glanced at Teeter and Kerrick and Holbrook. Then he stepped across the street and they went with him.

Sessler and Carney were standing three paces down the walk and Charlie went over to them. To Carney, Charlie said, "You didn't see Fred yet, huh?"

"I just couldn't do it," Carney said. "Call me what you want, but it wouldn't come off."

"Give me the check," Charlie said and held out his hand.

Carney smiled and handed it over. "I knew you'd help me."

"Why am I helping you?" Charlie asked.

"Because we're friends, in spite of it all." He hesitated. "Put the boy back in school. It's all right."

"Is it really?"

"Blame it on angry men," Carney said. "Like Paul says, times have changed. And we don't have to like everything we have to do. But I suppose in time, we'll learn to like it. Men don't unbend easy, Charlie. It's hard, painful work." Then he smiled. "But I envy you, Charlie. Yes, I'd even trade places with you. It must be good to be a man who isn't a prisoner of something, his conscience, or his hates. You're a leader now, Charlie. Lead them good, and maybe at the same time you can lead some of us." He reached out and slapped Charlie Two-Moon on the arm and walked across the street and down toward his office.

"He's a good doctor," Paul Sessler said. "Whether he's a good man or a bad one is in the point of view."

"Isn't that the way it is with everyone?"

"I suppose." He drew on the cigar, then made a face and shied it into the street. "That's a rotten smoke." He looked back over his shoulder at Allen's place. "It's a paradox of nature, of course, but it's always easier to get a man to do the wrong thing rather than what's right. You'll have to keep an eye on Allen, and some others in town. But you already know that." He laughed. "It's a twist, to be sure, but Allen really started this, didn't he? When he hit your cousin. Isn't that what got Kerrick going?"

"It was the last thing," Charlie said. "There's always something behind everything."

"Sure," Sessler said. "I hear you're going to get married."

Charlie smiled. "In ten days, before her folks go back."

"Are you going to change your name?"

"What? Why should I do that?"

Sessler shrugged. "Well, to be honest with you, I rather expected you to do that some time ago. I don't know how to say this, but you quit the reservation and rather shunned your relatives and—well, some men work damned hard to be someone they're not when their real value lies—well, you know what I'm talking about."

"Yes, I do," Charlie Two-Moon said. "Me change my name? To what? Smith? Simmons? Jones? Andrews?" He laughed and it was a lifted, free sound. "Me pure, 100 percent 'Merican Injun." Then he slapped Sessler on the back. "See you around," and trotted across the street to the hotel.

Sessler turned and saw George Grant standing in the doorway and Grant was looking across the street to Charlie Two-Moon, who was just going inside the hotel. Sessler said, "You saw that? Heard it? There's a good man, George."

Grant left the doorway and stood on the sidewalk beside Paul Sessler, and when he spoke his voice was soft. "This has been the best night of my life, I guess."

"Maybe it is for all of us, only we just don't know it," Sessler said and walked down the street to his car.

Center Point Large Print
600 Brooks Road / PO Box 1
Thorndike, ME 04986-0001 USA

(207) 568-3717

US & Canada:
1 800 929-9108
www.centerpointlargeprint.com